I pulled myself up the ladder to the roof.

"Do you want to explain your plan?" I asked Teddy.

"Did you read the comic?" he answered.

I read aloud: "'Fools! They take so many precautions to make sure they aren't being followed, but they never look up.'"

In the next panel, Nightowl dove from the edge of the roof to a gargoyle perched on the next building over. I peered over the eave to see the closest rooftop, which was at least fifteen feet away and twenty feet down.

"Are you planning to pursue her across the rooftops?" I asked.

Teddy looked around in disbelief. Then he lowered his head. "Sorry, I . . . "

I let out a groan of frustration. Then, as quickly as it had vanished, hope reappeared. About half a mile down the road, I saw Ms. Matthews's car change lanes.

I finally knew how I was going to track her.

READ THEM ALL!

#1: SECRET IDENTITY CRISIS

#2: FREEZER BURNED

by

JAKE BELL

cover and comic art by

CHRIS GIARRUSSO

SCHOLASTIC INC.

New York Toronto London Auckland

Sydney Mexico City New Delhi Hong Kong

For Taryn and Griffin
There's no such thing as "too smart."

ISBN: 978-0-545-15669-1

12 11 10 9 8 7 6 5 4 3 2 1 10 11 12 13 14 15/0

Printed in the U.S.A.
First printing, May 2010

Contents

Spreading Rumors About So-Called Superheroes

I can't think of anything really exciting that had happened during the first twelve years of my life. But that all started to change one morning in sixth grade.

My dad was watching the news while he got ready for work. That meant my sister and I were stuck watching it, too, while we ate our breakfast, even though I really wanted to watch Plastic Pup cartoons. Instead, I had to try to tune out all the boring talk about politics and the stupid jokes of Wally the Wacky Weatherman.

"Now back to our top story of the hour," the news anchor boomed in a deep, serious voice. "Yesterday afternoon, there was another sighting of what some people are calling—strange as it may sound—a superhero . . . right here in Kanigher Falls."

My head snapped up from my cereal bowl. For once, I was interested in the news.

"That's right," bubbled the blond coanchor. "Superheroes are common in big cities, like Kurtzburg, but Kanigher Falls hasn't seen a superhero since Jade Mask marshaled the Founders' Day parade twelve years ago."

As the video rolled, I leaned forward to get a better look. The footage was shaky and very blurry. A bank alarm rang shrilly, and two people ran out the front door of the bank, each carrying a grocery bag in one hand and a gun in the other. They jumped into a car that pulled away before they could even close their doors.

Whoever was working the video camera tried to zoom in on the license plate, but the car vanished from the screen. The image spun around as the camera operator tried to figure out what was happening. People started screaming.

The camera tilted up just in time to catch a shot of a purple boot and what could have been a purple skirt. Someone must have lifted the car at least twenty feet into the air, because the sound of shattering glass and twisting metal as it fell to the ground was deafening. The shaky camera work made it impossible to see any details, but a white and purple blur was definitely flying in front of the skyscrapers, carrying the two bank robbers.

The news anchor reported that the thieves had been deposited on the front steps of the Seventh Police

Precinct's station house. "Police would not confirm whether the apprehensions were made by Ultraviolet, the rumored superhero of Kanigher Falls," he continued. "However, several eyewitnesses—including the camera operator of the previous video clip—all swear they saw the woman."

They cut to a series of interviews with people who had seen the bank robbery. A little old lady pointed at the sky. "She picked up that car like it was no heavier than a toy," she croaked.

A fat man in a blue suit shook his head. "I'm not sure what I saw, but I know it was a woman wearing white and purple, just like I've heard about on the news."

I was shocked to see the next person being interviewed. It was Ms. Matthews, my history teacher. Underneath her image, the TV station had written *Sophie Matthews, Superhero Skeptic.* I watched as my sour-faced teacher rolled her eyes. I was pretty familiar with the expression. It was Ms. Matthews's way of telling someone he'd asked a really stupid question. I'd seen that look too many times, most recently when my friend Teddy had asked her why John Adams added a "Quincy" to his name the second time he became president.

"This is what you consider responsible journalism?" Ms. Matthews scoffed. "Spreading rumors about so-called superheroes? A bank was robbed and the criminals were brought to justice, but you're here stirring up silly comic-book fantasies." She clucked her tongue disapprovingly, the way she always did when Teddy . . . well, the way she always did when Teddy did pretty much anything.

"Isn't that your teacher?" my dad asked, gesturing toward the TV with his coffee mug.

"Yeah," I responded, my mouth full of Cocoa Blasters and milk.

"She's a barrel of laughs, isn't she?"

"She hates everything," I explained. "The class, the school, the students, and now even superheroes. The only thing that makes her happy is talking about boring old stuff, like . . . I don't know . . . " I looked down at the history notes sitting next to my backpack. I'd spent most of the lecture sketching a pretty cool picture of Freedom Knight beating up Painspider, just like in last month's issue of *Freedom Knight,* #342, but I had also managed to jot down a few points about the Civil War. I picked a few of the words at random. "Like slavery or the American Grant," I read aloud.

My dad stopped drinking his coffee and stared at me, confused. Then he looked down at my notes. "Do you mean *U. S.* Grant?"

"United States, American—you knew what I meant," I

said with a wave of my hand. "On the bright side, I only have to be in her class for an hour a day."

"U. S. Grant was a person, Nate, not a thing," my dad said sternly. "It's Ulysses S. Grant, not *United States* Grant."

"Whatever. What I was saying—"

"No, not 'whatever.' Nate, you're in sixth grade. You should know who President Grant was."

"Right." I wanted to talk my way out of looking stupid, but I couldn't think of anything to say. "Um . . . on a positive note, I got a B in gym."

My dad wasn't impressed.

"We're doing flash cards when I get home," he ordered. My dad never saw a pack of flash cards he didn't like. There were times I was certain the store owners in Kanigher Falls were purposely stocking boxes of flash cards at their checkout counters just in case my dad happened to shop there. He would come home from the hardware store and announce, "I got a Phillips-head screwdriver, eight sheets of medium-grit sandpaper, a box of one hundred multiplication flash cards, and a pack of C batteries." Seriously, what hardware store stocks math flash cards?

What made things worse was that my big sister, Denise, loved doing flash cards with Dad. She could recognize the faces of all the U.S. presidents — even Benjamin Harrison — before she was five. She knew her multiplication tables by the time she was six. If you named a year, she could rattle off any significant historical events that had taken place then, along with their dates.

"Okay," I said with a sigh. "Sorry, Dad."

"No need to be sorry," he chuckled. "Anytime's a good time for flash cards." Without warning, he wheeled around to face my sister. "Denise! Seventeen sixty-five!"

"Parliament passes the Stamp Act," she mumbled, rolling her eyes and slurping her cereal. "It was the first direct British tax on the American colonies, fueling separatist feelings that would eventually lead to the American Revolution."

"Very good!" Dad smiled, turning his back long enough for me to shoot her the evil eye and for her to stick her tongue out at me in reply.

By then the news anchor was done talking about anything I cared to hear, and was having a conversation with Gary Greenthumb the Garden Guru about peat moss. I grabbed my backpack, drank the last sip of my apple juice, and headed for the front door.

"I want to see your homework tonight before you watch any TV," my dad shouted as I tried to make my escape. "And I don't want to hear, 'The teacher didn't give us any'!"

It wasn't that my sister was smarter than me—

Well, okay, maybe my sister *was* smarter than me. The point was I knew plenty of things. They just weren't the things my teachers were grading me on.

For example, what other kid in my class knew that Mr. Enigma's first appearance was in *American Musketeers* issue twelve, much less owned a near-mint copy? Who among them could identify the colorist on a 1970s issue of *Man Ghost* just from the shading of the hero's shadow? Certainly none of them had ever won the prestigious Ultimate Comic Book Trivia Championship of Knowledge medal awarded every June at Funny Pages, the local comic-book shop. I knew because the last three were hanging in my bedroom.

And I knew my comic-book collection was bigger than those of any other three guys at school combined.

That was why I was so excited about having a superhero in town. Suddenly, everyone was talking about superheroes, and no one knew more about superheroes than me.

Growing up in Kanigher Falls had been difficult for me, since we'd never had a superhero. One eighth-grade kid was from Fradon, and he had his picture taken with

Ms. Miraculous two years ago, before his family moved here. If I had a quarter for every time he'd found a reason to "casually" pass that photo around and make sure everyone got a good look at it, I'd be able to afford that near-mint copy of *Marauder* #2 in the locked display case at Funny Pages. Mark Schweikert claimed to have seen Zilch at the mall in Claremont, but since Zilch is a shape-shifter and can look like anyone, it was kind of hard to prove. Wintertyrant had taken one of my classmates' uncles hostage during a standoff with police at the stock exchange the past summer, and another girl claimed that her grandmother's neighbor in Weisinger was Baron Shield.

Even my mom had stories. She'd grown up in Darwyn City, and she'd always seen Phantom Ranger when she was a kid. She made it sound like you couldn't turn the corner without bumping into the guy. Of course, when she and my dad got married, they didn't stay in Darwyn City. They had to move to boring old Kanigher Falls.

But now things were going to change. We finally had our own superhero.

Don't Wish for Supervillains

"Did you see her on TV?" Teddy asked as he ran down his driveway to meet me, nearly tripping over his untied sneakers. Every morning, Teddy seemed to be running late, no matter how early his mom tried to wake him.

"Yeah," I said. "She wears purple boots."

"I know," Teddy agreed. "I still can't tell whether she wears a cape, though."

"I'm pretty sure she wore one last time," I replied.

Last Thursday, the news had shown video footage from a mall parking lot security camera that showed a guy getting mugged while walking to his car. Just as the poor guy was handing over his wallet, the mugger vanished. A moment later, Ultraviolet handed the guy his wallet and then flew away.

She was on the screen for less than a second, but

the news station froze the image and enlarged it. The picture was grainy and blurry, but it was the closest thing anyone had to a photo of Ultraviolet. The next day, it was printed in the newspaper. I'd looked at the picture at least a thousand times and had reached the conclusion that she wore a cape and some kind of mask over her eyes. The security camera footage wasn't in color, but eyewitnesses all agreed that her outfit had been purple and white. Some people said she wore a skirt, and this morning's video seemed to confirm that. But it could have been part of a cape, so I wasn't positive.

"Unless she actually slows down long enough to talk to someone or let someone get a decent picture, we'll never really be sure," I said with a sigh.

"Do you think we'll ever see her?" Teddy asked as he ran his hands through his brown hair. Teddy never seemed to have time to comb it in the mornings.

"Most of the sightings have been downtown," I answered. "There aren't many banks or jewelry stores to be robbed around here, and I doubt she's going to swoop into Ditko Middle School to stop Meathead from stealing kids' milk money."

Rumor had it Meathead McCaskill made so much cash shaking down kids for their lunch money that the Internal Revenue Service had launched an investigation a few years earlier but had to drop it when they found out he was only fifteen.

"Maybe some weekend we can get my mom to drive us downtown and we can hang out near a bank and look for her or something," said Teddy.

"Banks downtown are closed on the weekends," I reminded him. "Besides, it's not like we can just stake out one bank. She's shown up all over the place. She can fly, and apparently she also has superspeed, so even if a bank got robbed one block away from where we were, she'd have the bad guys in custody before we could even cross the street."

"I guess you're right," Teddy said with a sad shrug. "What if we went to the hospital and hung out with your mom? Eventually, Ultraviolet would rescue somebody who needed to go to the emergency room for something."

My mom was an emergency room surgeon at Kanigher Falls General Hospital.

"I asked her, but she said no one's actually seen Ultraviolet yet," I told Teddy. "My mom said she's so fast that when she's dropped patients off, she's gone before anyone notices. Besides, my mom's way too busy to have us hanging around."

"Well . . ." Teddy struggled to think of another option. "Maybe a supervillain will attack the city and the fight will last long enough for us to get a good look at her," he suggested.

Don't get me wrong. Teddy is my best friend, and I feel bad for him when Ms. Matthews rolls her eyes at him, but sometimes he says things that are pretty stupid.

"Teddy, if my choice is between seeing a real, live superheroine or keeping Kanigher Falls supervillain free, I'm not going to wish for bad guys."

"Hmm. I hadn't thought of that."

"Apparently not."

When we reached the school crosswalk, a tall girl with short, dark hair and glasses was waiting for us. Fiona was always easy to pick out in a crowd, not only because of her height, but because she was the only girl in the school who'd be caught dead wearing a worn-out Man Ghost T-shirt and reading a tattered copy of *The Stupendous Shiningstar & Astro, Kid Genius.*

"Did you see her on the news?" Fiona asked excitedly. "She's wearing purple boots. They came up to just below the knee."

"We saw," Teddy said. "But don't go hoping super-villains will attack the school just so you can see her boots."

Fiona rolled her eyes. We continued the conversation as we waited for the Don't Walk sign to change.

Unfortunately, Brubaker Elementary School was right next to ours, which meant we were surrounded by a bunch of little kids who were also waiting for the light.

"That costume isn't something she just threw together," Fiona said. "If she has an outfit like that, it means she's been planning this for a while. It's not like she just got powers last week and decided to go out and become a crime fighter."

Finally, the light changed, and we all crossed the street. In front of the elementary school, Principal McKechnie was raising the flag.

After we got to the other side, a horn blared. Tires squealed. We turned back to see a tiny girl jump onto the sidewalk while a dump truck came to a stop just a few feet away from her. Two weeks earlier, construction had started on new condominiums a block down the road. The truck drivers tended to forget about the School Zone signs, and the sounds of horns and brakes had become normal.

As we turned back around, we nearly bumped into Ms. Matthews.

"Oops, sorry," Teddy said. "I didn't see you."

Ms. Matthews failed to acknowledge us at all. Instead, she watched with a sour look as the truck pulled away.

We walked around her and continued talking about that morning's news. That got her attention.

"Don't you have better things to think about?" she huffed. "This town needs to get over its ridiculous childish fantasy about flying women in purple capes saving the day."

She pushed her glasses further up on her nose. Sensing the oncoming lecture, I grabbed Teddy by the arm and hustled him away. Fiona was already a few steps ahead.

"I know three students who could go a long way toward saving themselves if they'd review chapter twelve of their history books before today's quiz!" Ms. Matthews shouted after us.

"What is her problem?" Teddy grumbled once we were out of earshot. "School hasn't even started and she's already yelling at us."

o o o

As it turned out, we should have listened to her advice. The quiz was so hard I doubted I had managed anything better than a C. But that wasn't until much later in the day, a day that proved to be one of the best I'd ever had, at least while school was in session. In math class, Mr. Reynolds asked a question about two trains heading toward each other at sixty miles an hour, and the discussion quickly turned into a debate about whether

Ultraviolet was strong enough to stop them from colliding. Then, in gym, we talked about the power needed to lift a car, and in science, we debated whether Ultraviolet's powers were the result of scientific experimentation, mutation, or technology.

Science was the best, because Dr. Content was as excited about superheroes as we were. His chalkboard was crammed full of data about Ultraviolet, and he scribbled down every little fact we could think of to share.

"She seems to show up more at night than during the day," someone suggested from the back of the classroom.

"Nighttime appearances," Dr. Content recited as he scribbled in one of the few bare spaces left on the board. "What does that tell us?"

"There's more crime at night?" Fiona asked.

"Or that her powers don't come from the sun!" another kid yelled. "Maybe she even gets them from the moon . . . like a werewolf!"

"It tells us she has a day job," Teddy said. This got a laugh from the class.

Dr. Content nodded in agreement. "Those are all good suggestions." He pointed at the jumbled list scrawled on the board and shrugged. "So how do we decide which of these observations are important and which are trivial? How do we determine which of these is the reason that we see her more at night? Maybe it's all three. Maybe it's a fourth reason. Maybe it just doesn't matter."

Dr. Content spread his arms wide with an excited flourish that sent his combed-over hair to the opposite side of his head. "This is where science comes in. At this point, we are merely speculating, but science forces us to take that speculation and explain it. If we can't justify our theories with facts, they get thrown out. If we observe something once but can't seem to observe it again, it gets thrown out. Science is repeatable. Understand?"

The lunch bell rang, but no one ever got up until Dr. Content finished speaking. He was a small man — not much larger than a few of the ninth graders — and some of the kids liked to laugh about how nerdy he was, but I think maybe those were the reasons he was one of the most popular teachers. While some teachers towered over us and delivered lectures as if the end of the world would be averted only if we knew how to divide fractions, this tiny man with thick-rimmed glasses and a nasal voice kept us hanging on to his every word. We usually found ourselves as interested in his lectures as he was.

"Back when I worked at the power plant, that was rule number one. Everything must be repeatable. When you're dealing with nuclear reactors, you can't bank on speculation. Well, that's all for today, class. We'll get back to geology tomorrow, so be sure to review the three types of rocks and what sets them apart from one another."

As I got up, he put his hand on my desk and asked me to stick around for a few minutes. I sat back down.

Once the rest of the students were gone, he began filing away papers in a folder that spread across his desk like an accordion.

"Nate, progress reports come out next week and I was looking over your grades," he began.

"I know I didn't do very good on the last test—"

"Very well, Nate," he corrected me. "You didn't do very *well* on the last test. But this isn't English class, right? My point is that I want to give you a chance to help yourself out."

I knew what was coming next. I was about to receive an offer of a lot of busy work in the form of "extra credit."

"How would you feel about taking on an extra-credit project?"

I sighed, weighing my need for extra points against the absolute boredom of sorting leaves and rocks into categories.

"What do you have in mind?" I asked warily.

He pointed at the board. "You like superheroes, right?" he asked. "Aren't you, like, Mr. Comic Book?"

I leaned forward in my seat. "Yeah," I replied. "How did you know that?"

"Funny Pages has your picture up behind the counter because you won a comic trivia game."

I nodded enthusiastically. "The Ultimate Comic Book Trivia Championship of Knowledge," I clarified. "What were you doing at Funny Pages?"

"Where else am I going to buy my comics in this town?" he replied with a smile. "What would you think of putting together a scientific report on Ultraviolet?"

My eyes and smile widened.

"I would expect you to employ the scientific method, which we've discussed in class, and give me a detailed report on anything you learn, whether it's who she is, where she came from, what powers she has and where she got them . . . anything, really. Then maybe you can present the report to the class."

I slumped back in my chair. There were few things in this world I hated more than public speaking. I got knots in my stomach just thinking about it. Two weeks ago, Mr. Dawson had asked me to read a Robert Frost poem called "Fire and Ice" aloud in English class, but I had barely made it through the first line before I'd had to sit down so I wouldn't throw up.

"I'm not very good at class presentations," I admitted.

"Stage fright?" he chuckled. "I suppose we could work around that. How about you make your presentation to me after class?"

That sounded good. I nodded.

"Okay." He looked at his calendar. "I'll give you until the end of the month, but I'd like you to give me updates at least once a week, just so I know you're making progress and you aren't going to slap the whole thing together the night before it's due. Fair enough?"

This teacher was offering me the chance to research superheroes to earn a better grade and he was asking if that was fair? Before he could change his mind, I jumped up and shook his hand.

"It's a deal!" I agreed.

Lunchroom Hero

I was convinced this was one of the greatest days ever, but somehow things managed to get even better during lunch—even with Ms. Matthews on lunch duty.

By the time I joined my friends, they were deeply engrossed in conversation while waiting to buy their lunches. Dave Bargman clearly wasn't on the Ultraviolet bandwagon. "She's no big deal," he insisted. "Phantom Ranger could beat her up anytime."

It wasn't a surprise that Dave would defend the superiority of Phantom Ranger. Even other superheroes—and no doubt a few supervillains—idolized the Ranger, the popular champion of Darwyn City.

Not only had Phantom Ranger been one of the world's greatest heroes since before my mom could walk—protecting one of the biggest cities in the country, mentoring up-and-coming heroes, and somehow always having time to stop and sign an autograph for his fans—but he also managed to do it all without any superpowers. That was why everyone loved him. Those of us who hadn't been born with superpowers could look at Phantom Ranger and believe that there was a chance we could be superheroes, too.

But as much as I loved Phantom Ranger, he was Darwyn City's hero, and now Ultraviolet was ours.

"You don't know that," Teddy retorted. "We don't know the extent of her powers yet."

"Also, why would Phantom Ranger *want* to fight Ultraviolet?" Fiona added.

Dave shook his head as if he couldn't believe she'd asked such a stupid question. "He would have to fight her if a supervillain with mind-control powers took over her brain!"

Robby Baker offered his opinion. "What if she turns out to be a supervillain who's hiding her true identity and pretending to be a hero so she can win the trust of the city and betray us when we least expect it?"

"Puh-leeze," Teddy groaned. "That hasn't happened in years. Not since Screamfang posed as Commander Cavalier."

For years, Screamfang had been a pretty hapless bad guy—with bad teeth—who lived down South. His power was being able to scream loudly enough to break glass. Once heroes realized that all they had to do was stuff a little cotton in their ears when he was around, Screamfang didn't last too long.

A few months after Wildblaze nabbed Screamfang for planning to blow up Buscema Dam and flood the city of Lenwein, a new hero, named Commander Cavalier, showed up in the town of Rosandru, a few miles away. Commander Cavalier dressed like one of the three musketeers, used a sword to fight criminals . . . and screamed really loudly. He was praised for being Rosandru's new champion, but after a few weeks, a mugger managed to punch Commander Cavalier in the mouth, knocking out his false teeth and revealing his fangs.

Eventually, it came to light that Screamfang had been planning to rob the Federal Reserve bank in Rosandru by earning the trust of the police and the community, then exploiting that trust to get inside the vault.

"Ultraviolet's not going to be another Screamfang," I assured Robby.

"You're just saying that because you don't want her to be," Dave said. "You're starstruck because Kanigher Falls has never had a superhero. I lived in Haney until I was seven, so I'm used to being around superhe—"

"Haney?" I laughed. "You're not used to being around superheroes; you're used to Captain Zombie."

Captain Zombie was a prime example that not all heroes were great heroes. Haney's hometown hero was a zombie who had the ability to talk to other zombies and was instilled with the "Power of the Graveyard," whatever that meant. For the most part, it meant that as long as you didn't commit any crimes within a block or two of the Haney County Cemetery, he was more or less powerless to stop you.

Everyone chuckled for a moment, but the laughter died down as the cafeteria doors opened and Meathead McCaskill walked in, ready for work.

Meathead stood a full head taller than anyone else in the lunch line. Being three years older will do that. Most kids his age were getting their first jobs and driver's licenses, but Meathead was still struggling to get past eighth grade.

Actually, there was much debate about just how hard Meathead was struggling. The rumor was that he'd failed third, fifth, and seventh grades for business purposes. He'd been strong-arming kids out of their lunch money for years, and it had proven quite lucrative.

He stomped his way down the line, examining everyone who was waiting to buy lunch. We all knew what was coming and, worse, knew we were defenseless to prevent it. He zeroed in on a group right behind us. Witnessing him confidently striding up to them was like watching one of those wildlife documentaries about a lion stalking a pack of zebras. You knew what was going to happen. You knew it was going to get ugly. You knew someone was going to get hurt.

Yet you couldn't look away.

It wasn't that we didn't want to help the other kids, but we couldn't. Standing up to Meathead would get you three black eyes—two now and another in a month as a reminder not to cross him ever again.

Meathead closed in, towering over the four boys. He held his hand out. "You know the drill, guys."

Without question, three of them placed their lunch money in his hand, their shoulders hunched in anticipation of a long, hungry afternoon. The last kid, a freckled, skinny boy with orange hair, started sweating, his eyes darting back and forth.

"What's the problem?" Meathead asked impatiently.

"M-my . . . uh . . . my mom found out I've been having my lunch money stolen," he stammered. "So she bought me a lunch ticket instead of giving me cash."

Meathead was unhappy.

"I . . . I tried to tell her you wouldn't like that, but she wouldn't listen to me," he continued sheepishly.

"You're going to have to bring me twice as much money tomorrow," Meathead growled.

"But my mom's not going to give me money when she already paid for—"

"Don't worry. I know the perfect way to convince your mom," Meathead assured him as he made a fist. The boy cringed, but the punch never landed.

Ms. Matthews stood behind Meathead, her hand gripping his wrist.

"Is there a problem, Angus?" she asked Meathead.

"No," he answered flatly. "No problem at all. I was just talking to Alan here. He's my neighbor and his mom told me to babysit him after school."

"That's nice," she replied. I could tell she wasn't buying his story. "These younger students are lucky to have you around, especially since you're buying their lunches." Ms. Matthews pointed to the cash in Meathead's hand.

I'd never seen Meathead so helpless before. The guy might not have been the smartest kid in school—he may well have been the dumbest—but he had enough brains to know he'd been caught red-handed. Playing along was his only way out without being suspended.

He handed back the money and smiled at Ms. Matthews. He tried to smile at the kids, too, but it looked more like a scowl. "Tell your moms I was happy to help you out, and maybe they should give you the money to *pay me back* tomorrow."

"I wouldn't worry about that, Angus," Ms. Matthews insisted as she released his wrist. She turned to the rest of the guys in line, looking them each in the eye. But her voice rose several decibels, making it clear she was addressing all of us. "From now on, I don't want to see Angus here having to *buy anyone else's lunches*, which is what I'll assume he's doing whenever I see him approaching people in the cafeteria line with large sums of money in his hands." She turned her gaze to Meathead. "Is that understood?"

Meathead nodded in agreement. Looking unsure of where to go, he remained standing with the same group of guys while Ms. Matthews returned to monitoring the lunchroom for any other rule breakers.

All at once, a hundred conversations suddenly picked up where they'd left off moments earlier. Robby and Dave continued our discussion on superheroes, but I don't know whether any of us were really paying attention. Having personally handed over more than seventy-eight dollars in cash, and having brown-bagged my lunches from fifth grade on just to avoid lunch-line confrontations with Meathead, I couldn't take my eyes off the bully.

"You got something to say, Banks?"

"Payback," I muttered under my breath. Unfortunately, I said it more loudly than I'd meant to.

Meathead puffed up like some bizarre fish you see only in zoos or on nature shows. Then he threw his arms out to the sides and took a step toward me. His face reddened. He pulled his lips away from his teeth, exposing them the way an angry bear does before mauling whomever has been stupid enough to get between it and a fat, tasty salmon.

I instinctively stepped backward, bumping into my friends. "I meant that you said those guys could pay you back, so Ms. Matthews should have said something about payback."

Meathead didn't come any closer, but he didn't back off, either.

"You know, like 'Oh, you'll get your payback when you least expect it,' or 'I'm sure you'll get what's owed to you,'" I mumbled. "Something like Phantom Ranger would say."

He sneered and turned away. "Phantom Ranger," he scoffed. "Grow up, you comic-book geek."

There are those who say that names can hurt as

much as fists. Those people have never been punched by Meathead McCaskill. I, for one, counted myself lucky to get away with only a halfhearted insult hurled in my direction as he slunk away.

Teddy and Fiona finished paying for their lunches and we filed outside to eat. When we couldn't find room for all three of us at any of the picnic tables, we chose a shady spot beneath an elm tree near the soccer field, on the fringe of the lunch area.

"You could see his brain short-circuiting." Fiona snickered. "He couldn't hit her, he couldn't take her money, and I guess he doesn't know how to do anything else."

"Who'd have thought an uptight teacher would be such a big hero?" said Teddy. "I just may start doing my history homework after all."

"No, you won't," Fiona said with a giggle.

I took a deep breath and looked at the sky. As I looked up, I recognized something in the clouds.

A purple and white streak zipped overhead, at least five hundred feet above the school. I couldn't begin to guess how fast it was moving, but I feel safe saying I'd never seen any plane move that quickly.

It had to be Ultraviolet.

I've Never Seen a Superhero Before

The blur stopped over the neighborhood across the street from our school, then took a ninety-degree turn, heading straight for the ground.

Ultraviolet was just a block away!

I sprang to my feet and stared intently across the street. My friends were suddenly hundreds of miles away—or at least they seemed to be. Fiona noticed that I was distracted.

"Nate, what are you looking at?" she asked.

"Tell me you both saw that," I pleaded, not taking my eyes from the spot where she'd disappeared.

"Saw what?" Teddy asked.

"I didn't see anything," Fiona agreed.

"It was her," I whispered.

"You want to give us a little more to go on, Nate?" Teddy urged. "'Her' could be a lot of people."

"Ultraviolet," I blurted. "She was flying over the school and she landed over there!" I gestured wildly, pointing out the path the purple and white streak had taken across the sky.

"I didn't see any—" Teddy said, but I cut him off.

"We need to go over there!" I exclaimed. "Now!"

Just a few hours earlier, I'd been explaining to Teddy that we could never catch up to Ultraviolet, even if she was only a block away, yet I couldn't convince my legs of the same thing. Before I realized it, I was sprinting across the soccer field, my eyes fixed on the roof behind which she'd disappeared.

Something colossal had to be happening just a few hundred yards away. Maybe a house was on fire or some nefarious criminal syndicate was operating across the street from Ditko Middle School. Whatever it was, I'd been waiting my entire life to see a real, live superhero in action, and nothing was going to stop me now.

"Where are you going?" Fiona shouted after me. But I didn't look back. I was afraid if I took my eyes off the spot where Ultraviolet had landed, I might miss seeing her fly away.

Leaving the soccer field, I dashed past the flagpole and through the faculty parking lot toward the street. I still hadn't seen the purple streak rocket over the rooftops again, so I knew there was still a chance to see Ultraviolet if—

"Where do you think you're going?" a voice shouted from across the parking lot. "Nathan Banks! Stop right where you are!"

It's a well-known fact among adults that nothing gets a kid's attention faster than calling him by his full name. My body instinctively stopped in its tracks.

Any other teacher might have been swayed if I had told him or her that Ultraviolet was across the street. Dr. Content might have even joined me on my quest. But unfortunately, the voice belonged to Ms. Matthews.

"You know students aren't allowed off campus during school hours," she snapped. "Return to the lunch area *immediately.*"

I was torn between my desire to keep running and my desire not to spend the rest of the school year in detention. It might not seem like much of a decision, but at that moment, I was telling myself that even if I got expelled, there were two other middle schools in Kanigher Falls I could go to. On the other hand, this might be my only chance ever to see a superhero in person.

Ms. Matthews made the decision for me as she stepped between me and the street. "What do you think you're doing, Nate?" she asked, her mouth puckered as though she'd been sucking a lemon.

"I—I saw . . . um, something over there," I stammered, pointing behind her.

"Something? Would you care to be more specific?"

I took a deep breath and looked her in the eye. I decided to take the plunge and tell her the truth. What came out was one long babbling sentence.

"I saw Ultraviolet, the superhero from the news—the one you saw yesterday—and she's doing something in that neighborhood right across the street and I have to see her because I've never seen a superhero before and all these other kids who grew up in bigger cities have seen guys like Phantom Ranger and Doctor Nocturne and even Captain Zombie, but I've never seen anyone and nobody knows more about superheroes than I do, so I really wanted to go see her before she flies away again so please just let me go."

For a moment, Ms. Matthews's face softened while she weighed my words.

"Please, Ms. Matthews," I said. "I know I'm not the smartest student and I'm not the best behaved, but I've never wanted anything as much as this, and I promise I will study and be quiet and pay attention during class. . . ."

She leaned forward, her glasses perched on the end of her nose. "You have exactly one minute to get back to the lunch area before you get detention."

My heart sank. Part of my brain was still screaming at me that I could outrun her. After all, if I couldn't outrun a history teacher wearing a skirt, maybe I didn't deserve to witness superheroics.

"I assure you there aren't any silly heroes there," she said. "Now turn around, Nathan, and go." I slowly pivoted and started walking back toward the lunch area.

But then, suddenly, something else came over me. A burst of adrenaline coursed through me as I took off running toward the parking lot again. I surprised myself almost as much as I seemed to surprise my teacher. I thought if I wove between the cars, I might be able to put enough distance between Ms. Matthews and me for me to make a break for it.

I wasn't thinking that for long.

I'd like to say I got about three steps before Ms. Matthews snatched the back of my shirt, but it would probably be too much to suggest I got a step and a half. It was amazing how quickly she was on top of me, like a leopard pouncing on an old, lame antelope.

The shot of adrenaline was gone. I was like one of those antelope, helpless and in complete shock. I halfheartedly tried to break free, but her grip was viselike. It was clear I was going nowhere.

That's not entirely accurate. I *was* going somewhere, but it was nowhere I wanted to be. Ms. Matthews's grasp on my shirt loosened, her other hand came down on my shoulder, and she pointed me straight toward the principal's office.

Maybe You Should Actually READ a Few Comics

What had been the best day ever quickly deteriorated as I sat across from Principal Gwynn, listening to him explain why students are not allowed off campus and tell me how disappointed he was in me for openly defying a teacher. He had no interest in my story about Ultraviolet. By the time I got out of his office, I just felt lucky not to have been suspended.

As if things weren't bad enough, I had to pick up a late pass and make my way as quickly as possible to history class, where I would face Ms. Matthews again.

It would be in my best interest, I decided, to keep my head down and my mouth shut. So I quietly settled into my seat, doing my best not to make eye contact with Ms. Matthews. In an effort to stay out of trouble, I reached into my backpack and pulled out a stack of comics, all safely preserved in plastic bags with acid-free cardboard backings to keep the pages from yellowing. I figured I could just read my comics quietly while Ms. Matthews droned on and on about the Spanish-American War. It was what I did during most of Ms. Matthews's history classes.

I carefully opened a near-mint copy of *Hurricane Squad* #24 while Ms. Matthews described Theodore Roosevelt leading a charge up San Juan Hill.

It was a pretty good issue. The Squad had to rescue a group of intergalactic surveyors from an alien commando team, but Sisteroid almost had to remain behind, because her boss suspected her secret identity. She managed to throw him off by tripping over a chair and pretending she'd twisted her ankle, which was something so klutzy her boss would never expect it from an incredibly coordinated superhero.

Just as I was fully engrossed in the story, I sensed Ms. Matthews standing over me. I closed the comic and looked up at her without saying a word, figuring anything I might say or do would likely just get me in more trouble. After a moment of silence, she reached down and picked up one of the comics from my desk.

She held it between her thumb and index finger at arm's length, the way you would pick up a dead fish or a stinky gym sock. Then she scooped the entire stack of comics off my desk and turned to face the class. "Please put your books away," she announced. "It's quiz time!"

Two hours later, I was headed back to Ms. Matthews's room for detention when Dr. Content stopped me in the hallway. "Mr. Banks," he greeted me. "I hear you've had a busy day. Word in the teachers' lounge is that you were trying to do some off-campus research for your extra-credit project."

He smiled sympathetically, but I was in no mood to smile back.

"Oh, I'm sorry," he said. "I didn't mean to joke."

I stopped just outside Ms. Matthews's classroom and looked around carefully before I spoke. "I saw her, Mr. Content—"

"Doctor Content," he corrected me.

"Right, sorry," I said. "I saw her, Dr. Content. Nobody believes me, but I saw her."

His eyes brightened and he leaned toward me. "Nobody believed Copernicus, Nate. If you went back in time and told people dying of influenza that what was making them sick were tiny things called germs—organisms so small they couldn't even see them—and that their lives could be spared by washing their hands with soap a few times a day, you'd probably be burned at the stake for being a witch. What matters is that you are correct, not that people *think* you're correct."

I started to smile, but the door to Ms. Matthews's room suddenly swung open behind me. "Nathan, you are late," Ms. Matthews said. Slowly, she turned to face Dr. Content. "Malcolm, I would appreciate your not keeping one of my students on my time."

Dr. Content smiled and stepped back. "I apologize, Sophie. I was just discussing an extra-credit project with Nate."

I hustled into my seat.

"What did the criminal mastermind do, anyway?"

Ms. Matthews snorted impatiently. "If you must know, he went to the principal's office because he'd tried to leave campus during lunch; then when he finally got to class, he was reading comic books. Honestly, if all this foolishness about real superheroes isn't enough . . . what's the point of fictional ones?"

"The news will tell you Doctor Nocturne caught some smugglers in Kurtzburg, but you can't tag along and watch him in action," Dr. Content pointed out. "Comics let you see behind the scenes and understand what superheroes' lives must be like."

"Except that it's all fictionalized garbage," Ms. Matthews remarked.

“Some of it, sure,” Dr. Content agreed. “But a lot of it is probably more true than not.”

“You think comics are real?”

Dr. Content grinned. “Not the comics themselves, but some of the details.”

“Please tell me you’re not touting the educational value of comic books,” Ms. Matthews said with a sigh.

“All I’m saying is that everyone has something they do to escape their mundane life.” His voice dropped to nearly a whisper but was still loud enough for me to hear. “Maybe you should actually *read* a few comics before you write off a kid for liking them. Who knows? Maybe you’ll learn a thing or two.”

Ms. Matthews stiffened at the suggestion. “I have a lot of papers to grade, Dr. Content,” she said, dismissing him. “If you’ll excuse me . . .”

Dr. Content shot me a smile before backing away. Ms. Matthews shut the door and took a seat at her desk.

With my comics gone, I had nothing to do but stare blankly at the front of the classroom while Ms. Matthews graded some papers, occasionally sighing disappointedly or clucking her tongue in dismay. Neither of us spoke for what seemed like hours, but when I glanced at the clock, I realized it had been only around eight minutes.

Finally, Ms. Matthews finished grading and looked up at me, taking the stack of comics from her desk drawer.

"Who is Mang Host?" she asked.

I had no idea what she was talking about, but I assumed it was some history question I had answered wrong on our last quiz. I debated whether to take a weak stab at the answer—a Chinese emperor seemed like the safest guess—or just shrug and admit I had no idea. I opted for the shrug.

She held up one of the comics. "This *is* your comic, right?"

I looked at the cover. "That's Man Ghost," I corrected her. "They should probably put a dash between the two words or make the 'G' a little bigger."

She reexamined the cover and gave a small grunt as she walked toward my desk. "So, what does Man Ghost do?"

There was no condescension in her voice. She was actually asking me about comics without insulting me or complaining about how stupid superheroes were.

"He's just a ghost," I explained. "He can walk through walls and turn invisible and fly. He's kind of like a detective who solves crimes by sneaking around and hiding in places where people can't see him and stuff."

"Isn't that illegal?"

"Technically, yeah," I replied. "A few months ago they did a story where the police commissioner tried to get Man Ghost to officially join the police, but he had to turn down the offer. If Man Ghost was deputized by the police, he'd be violating the Fourth Amendment."

She shook her head in disbelief. "The Fourth Amendment?"

"Yeah," I said. "Man Ghost's inspections would be illegal searches, and the evidence would be inadmissible in court."

Ms. Matthews laughed. "Nathan, can you explain how it is that you just demonstrated a fairly thorough understanding of the Fourth Amendment and court procedure, yet I can't seem to convince you that Lincoln's Gettysburg Address is not where he got his mail during the Civil War?"

In my own defense, I knew that wasn't the right answer when I wrote it on my last history quiz, but I thought it was funny. And since I didn't know the right answer, I decided it was a decent guess.

"You have all these facts about comics and superheroes locked up in that brain of yours, but if I ask you to name the states that seceded from the Union in 1861, you'll tell me it's too difficult," she continued.

"But I can't remember all those—"

"There were only eleven states, Nate," Ms. Matthews said. She seemed a little exasperated with me. "But I'm sure if I asked you to name eleven superheroes and the cities they patrol, you could do it in a heartbeat."

"Phantom Ranger's in Darwyn City," I began. "Baron Shield's in Weisinger. Doctor Nocturne is in Kurtzburg. Lady Bullet— "

"See?" she interrupted. "That's my point. You obviously know a lot about superheroes and comics. I just think there might be more productive outlets for your efforts. True, there are a few—very few—people out there with superpowers. But most people—people like your parents, for example—have to get up every morning and figure out a way to put food on the table and pay the bills without the benefits of invulnerability or superstrength or flying. Maybe you should stop daydreaming about flying women and recognize how lucky you are to be surrounded by people who do much more than this Ultraviolet clown and don't get nearly the credit they deserve."

My mouth dropped open. Suddenly, I understood. "You're jealous," I said with a gasp.

"Wh-what?" she stammered in disbelief.

"You're jealous because everyone's talking about Ultraviolet and no one cares about your lectures or the next quiz you're going to spring on us. You want to be famous like she is—"

"I assure you I am *not* jealous of Ultraviolet, and I don't want to be famous," she replied firmly.

"You think you're making the world a better place by making us memorize when Grover Cleveland was elected president while heroes like Ultraviolet are saving lives every day."

She shook her head at me. Then she stood and gestured toward the clock. "Your time's up," she said with a sigh. "You're free to go."

I got up and slung my backpack over my shoulder. I wanted to ask for my comics back, but I decided that the best plan at that point was to get out of there as quickly as possible.

I Think My Teacher Is a Superhero

Teddy called me that evening to ask if I'd watched the news. I had—and I'd heard the story about Ultraviolet saving a dozen people from a burning office building that afternoon. There wasn't any new video, though, and there was nothing about what she'd done in the neighborhood across from school, so it must not have been too notable.

We didn't talk for long. Teddy had nothing to add to the conversation beyond repeating what the news had reported, and besides, I was preoccupied with what Ms. Matthews had said. Maybe I *was* too obsessed with superheroes. A simple two-second sighting had plunged me into what could only be described as temporary insanity. Looking back on what I'd done, I was embarrassed—and not just because I'd gotten caught. Maybe I needed to rethink my priorities.

I knew I had to take my schoolwork more seriously. I settled down on the couch, my backpack full of unfinished homework at my feet, and a box of Dad's infamous flash cards on the coffee table. I picked them up and began reviewing my multiplication tables.

"Very nice." Denise chuckled from the doorway after I'd gone through a dozen cards. "Keep up the good work and soon you'll be as smart as I was when I was six."

Flash cards may be a great educational tool, but they can serve many purposes. For example, a full deck can shut up a smart-mouthed older sister, or so I figured as I hurled the box at Denise's head. Luckily for her, my aim wasn't much better than my arithmetic.

ooo

The following day, I tried to maintain my commitment and focus, telling myself I wasn't going to talk about Ultraviolet or think about superheroes. That commitment lasted about twenty minutes.

It really wasn't my fault, though. I had an extra-credit assignment that required me to talk and think about Ultraviolet. On top of that, it was Friday, and that was the day of the week Teddy, Fiona, and I always went to Funny Pages to buy our new comics for the weekend. If I was going to stop being obsessed with superheroes, it would have to wait until the next week.

Shockingly, even Ms. Matthews seemed to have developed an interest in Ultraviolet. During history class, she dropped a reference to the previous day's office-building fire when lecturing about the Great Chicago Fire. When we were dismissed, she even stopped me to return the comics she'd confiscated the day before.

When the final bell rang at the end of the day, I met Teddy and Fiona near the football field, where the school's track-and-field team was practicing.

"Didn't you ask your new girlfriend if she wanted to come and buy some comics, too?" Fiona teased. She gestured to the faculty parking lot next to the football field. Ms. Matthews was walking toward a green car, but luckily she was out of earshot.

"Why should she buy her own when this guy will just let her take his?" Teddy joked.

"Shut up, Teddy." I laughed, shoving him playfully as we cut across the track, weaving through a pack of football players running laps in full pads.

As soon as we set foot on the grass inside the track, we heard a loud roar.

"Get off the field!" Coach Howard bellowed. He gestured that we should clear out.

We ignored him. He was used to our taking a shortcut through his Friday practices on the way to the comic-book store. He heaved a deep sigh of frustration and turned back to one of his players.

"Did Ms. Matthews give you back the comics she took or are you going to have to buy replacements?" Fiona asked.

"She was in a good mood . . . this time," I replied. "The one thing I learned is that I'm never taking my comics anywhere near that classroom ever again." I told them about how Ms. Matthews had been reading all my comics and asking lots of questions. "I just know that when she was reading them, she was probably bending the spines. Who knows what shape they're in now?" I paused and knelt down to open my backpack and inspect my comics.

"Aw, did the big mean lady get fingerprints all over your mint-condition copy of *Sergeant Stripes*?" Teddy teased as he and Fiona continued to walk across the field.

"No! No! No!" Coach Howard shouted. But this time, he wasn't yelling at us. He was barking at his quarterback, who had just unleashed a long pass down the sideline.

I looked up and couldn't help admiring the perfectly spiraling ball for a moment. Then I realized that it was headed right toward me. Worse, so were a wide receiver and two defensive backs, all looking up to track the ball and completely oblivious to my presence.

I was about to be the centerpiece in a collision of five hundred pounds of fast-moving athletes, helmets, and pads. I tried to get away, but I stumbled and couldn't get my legs under me.

Something flashed in front of me. I know it's a cliché when people say their life flashes before them the moment they think they're going to die, but I definitely saw a flash.

In the next second, I felt myself being yanked backward by the straps of my backpack. Then I heard the smack of helmets and pads smashing together and the dull thud of the football landing in the grass beside me. Standing behind me, her hand still wrapped tightly around my backpack straps, was Ms. Matthews.

The flash I'd seen hadn't been my life passing before my eyes. It had been my history teacher's arm reaching out to grab me with the same awesome quickness she'd used to stop me in the parking lot the day before.

"Are you okay, Nate?" she asked. I tried to stand, but I must have twisted my ankle when Ms. Matthews yanked me up onto my feet.

"I'll see if the school nurse is still here," she said. "If she's not, I'll call your parents to pick you up." I nodded silently. I was still in shock. But my friends seemed even more shaken up than I was.

"Are . . . are y-you okay?" Teddy stammered.

"Why?" I asked.

Fiona pointed to one of the defensive backs, who stood with his hands on his thighs, still looking a bit woozy from the hit, despite his protection. "You almost got your head torn off!" she shouted.

"But I didn't," I pointed out. "Ultraviolet saved me."

"Uh-oh," Teddy said to Fiona. "He's lost his mind." He knelt down in front of me, looking into my eyes and speaking loudly and clearly, enunciating each word. "Nate, you are in shock. That was not Ultraviolet. That was Ms. Matthews."

"No," I said. "I think it was both."

My friends stared at me blankly. I grinned.

"Ms. Matthews *is* Ultraviolet."

Did You Sprain Your Ankle or Your Brain?

Mom pulled my ankle close to her face about as gently as a rhinoceros trying to wash fine china. She twisted it one way, then the other.

"There's no bruising or swelling," she declared. "You're fine." She dropped my leg back onto the bed roughly.

"It hurts," I protested.

"You'll live. Now get up and help your dad with the yard. I have to get to work."

"Don't they teach you bedside manner in med school?" I groaned, rolling over and getting tangled in my sheets.

"Sure, but I don't want to use it all up on you," she said with a laugh. "I have a full day ahead of me. Lying in bed all day isn't going to make your foot feel better, so go mow the lawn."

My ankle did hurt, but that wasn't why I wanted to

stay in bed. After my brush with death the previous afternoon, my friends had dismissed my realization about Ms. Matthews as delusional ramblings. I needed rest, they insisted, but the longer I rested, the more certain I became that I was right.

Ms. Matthews had been in the parking lot when that quarterback had thrown the ball. It was weird that she had made her way across the field so quickly and tossed me aside like I weighed nothing at all. But until I could wrap my brain around the facts, I didn't dare discuss it with anyone, especially not my friends.

"What if I have internal injuries?" I shot back at my mom. "Did you ever think of that?"

Mom got a grim look on her face as she sat at the foot of my bed. "I hadn't thought about that," she said. "I was just reading a medical journal that said internal ankle injuries account for seventy percent of all ankle-related fatalities."

"Okay, okay," I groaned as I sat up.

"I don't know what I'd do if I found out that you had died of a misdiagnosed internal ankle injury," Mom cried melodramatically. "Especially not if you died before the lawn got mowed and I . . . and I — " She sniffled deeply.

"I'm getting up, so you can cut it out," I told her.

"And *I* had to do it tomorrow!" she fake-sobbed into her hands.

"You're hilarious, Mom."

"Hey, you should feel honored," she said brightly. "Most of my patients just get a diagnosis. Very few get the floor show."

I got up from the bed and stumbled on the sore ankle, reaching out a hand to steady myself on the dresser.

Mom smiled reassuringly. "You'll be fine. It's just going to be a little stiff because you haven't moved it all night. Walk around, work in the yard, go to the comic shop—pretty soon you'll forget all about it." She looked at her cell phone and stood up. "Okay, Nate, I'll see you tonight. I should be home before you go to bed."

For a moment, I considered sharing my theory about Ultraviolet. If anyone would understand, she would. She'd met Phantom Ranger more times than she could count. But I knew she was running late, so I gave her a small wave instead. Still leaning on the dresser, I put on some old clothes for working in the yard.

Mom was right. After an hour of pushing the lawn mower and trimming the bushes, I had forgotten about my ankle—at least until Teddy and Fiona rode up on their bikes.

“You finished yet?” Teddy asked as he came to a stop.

“Just about,” I replied.

“We figured you'd be ready and waiting for us,” Fiona said. “My game went long.” She was still wearing her soccer uniform.

“They lost again,” Teddy said.

“It wasn't my fault,” Fiona snapped.

“This time,” Teddy added with a laugh. Fiona punched him in the arm, which I thought he kind of deserved.

“Come on, Nate,” Teddy said as he rubbed his arm. “I was willing to wait a whole extra day for new comics, but a man has his limits.”

“I don't know if I want to go,” I said.

“What?” Fiona asked incredulously. “Did you sprain your ankle or your brain? Get your bike and let's go buy some comic books.”

I pushed the mower back to the garage and got out my bike, shouting to let my dad know where I was going. Dad nodded, waved to Teddy and Fiona, and went back to pulling weeds.

It was a bright, sunny afternoon, but you'd never have known that inside Funny Pages. The owner, Jeff, had covered all the windows with posters, most of which had faded in years of direct sunlight. Once you walked through the door, it was hard not to feel like a lab rat. But instead of cheese at the end of the maze, there was the rack of new releases.

Scattered throughout the labyrinth were some of the regular customers, reading comics. If they had real names, we never knew them. Inside the shop, they were known by names like Blubbs, Stench, 20 Questions, and Horse.

Jeff said hi to us as we walked in, and then went back to ringing up a customer I'd never seen before. I flipped through the copies of *Nightowl* on the rack, looking for a pristine one. Once I found a cover that showed not even the slightest scratch, wrinkle, or ding, I moved on to the stack of *Spin Doctors.*

As I approached the counter with two perfect specimens, I noticed a gray-haired man smiling at me as if we were old friends. I had a strange feeling that maybe I *did* know him from somewhere. Was he one of my dad's clients? Or one of the doctors who worked with my mom? Was he expecting me to recognize him and say hello?

He must have sensed my unease, because he shook his head apologetically. "I'm sorry," he said. "You look familiar."

"Probably from right here." Jeff slapped a photo

hanging on the wall behind the counter. It was a picture of me wearing a gold medal—or at least a medal coated in gold spray paint. "This is our Ultimate Comic Book Trivia Champion of Knowledge."

The older man chuckled, staring at the photo. "I had forgotten all about the Ultimate Comic Book Trivia Championship of Knowledge," he said nostalgically. "Wow, that takes me back."

"You know, you could enter the contest again," Jeff told the man. "It's open to everyone."

"No," the man said politely. "I won't be able to make it this year." Then he pointed at my copy of *Nightowl* on the counter. "You're going to like that issue. I let a friend read my copy, but she crumpled it up, so I had to buy a replacement."

As the man left, Teddy nudged me with his elbow. "His friend sounds like she'd get along with Ms. Matthews," he snickered.

"Don't you mean Ultraviolet?" Fiona said, laughing. "You probably don't remember after what happened yesterday, but you were going on and on about how Ms. Matthews was Ultraviolet."

"I remember," I assured her.

"Oh." She stopped laughing. "I didn't mean to make fun of you. It's just—"

I turned and walked out of the store, ignoring Jeff's good-bye. This was exactly what I'd wanted to avoid. It was bad enough that my friends thought my idea was worthy of jokes. I certainly wasn't going to let them make fun of me in front of grown men named Stench and Blubbs.

"Hey, Banks," grunted a familiar voice.

Slowly, I turned to see Meathead sidling up the sidewalk from a few stores down the strip mall.

"Looks like it's payback time," he announced. "Or time for back pay or time to pay me back or something like Phantom Ranger would say, huh?"

"I don't kn—" I began.

"Give me your lunch money, Banks."

I was taken aback. "I don't—um . . . You realize it's Saturday, right?"

"Cut the crap and hand over the money," he growled, thrusting his upturned palm toward my face and rapidly clenching and unclenching his fingers.

"It's Saturday," I persisted. "Nobody gets lunch money on Saturday."

Teddy and Fiona came out of the store.

"Well, then give me any money," Meathead said, conceding.

"Not to state the obvious, but we just came out of a

store," I said, pointing to Funny Pages. "We just spent all our money."

Cautiously, Meathead lowered his empty hand and thought over what I'd said. "Okay, I'm going to let you go this time," he agreed. "But next time I'm not going to be so nice."

He turned and strode away.

"What was that about?" Fiona asked.

"I guess if he can't mug people in the lunchroom anymore, he has to find new turf," I explained.

"No, I mean what was with the way you stormed out while we were still paying for our comics?" she said, clarifying.

"Oh. That."

"I didn't mean to joke about you almost getting hit by—"

"It's not that," I interrupted. With a deep breath, I got on my bike and started pedaling. Both my friends kept up alongside me. "I spent a lot of time last night thinking about it, and I still think . . . I think Ms. Matthews has superpowers."

Teddy swerved and narrowly missed hitting a parked car. I explained that she hadn't been on the field, that she'd moved so quickly, and that she was strong, but they weren't buying it.

"She must have been there," Teddy insisted. "We just didn't see her. She was behind us."

"And there are all kinds of stories about people getting bursts of strength or speed in emergency situations," Fiona reminded me.

"Maybe you're right," I admitted. "But I need to know for sure. If she is a superhero, I'm going to find a way to prove it."

Not the Best Plan: Not Even a Good Plan

On Monday afternoon, I stood between Teddy and Fiona outside the school, in front of the teachers' lounge.

Teddy looked up at the window and then back at me. "So you want us to just stand here and stare at this window all day in case Ultraviolet flies through it," he said.

"That's the idea," I confirmed.

"You had all day Sunday and this is what you came up with?" Fiona asked, annoyed.

"I know it's not the best plan—" I said.

"No, it's not," Fiona agreed. "I don't think anyone would even say it's a *good* plan, much less *the best.* Why didn't you call me? I could have come up with a better plan than this. Heck, even Teddy could have come up with something better."

"Thank you, Fiona," Teddy said smugly, unaware

that she'd just insulted him. "But let's give him one more chance. Run this by me again, Nate."

"Okay, Ms. Matthews has to change into Ultraviolet somewhere, right? Let's say she's sitting at her desk, grading papers, when she hears a little girl scream across town."

"You don't know she has superhearing," Fiona pointed out.

"This is just a theory, okay?" I continued. "Ms. Matthews closes her grade book, stands up, and walks calmly to the teachers' lounge, where she changes into her purple and white Ultraviolet uniform—"

"Wait, you think she just changes right in the middle of the teachers' lounge?" Fiona interrupted.

"I don't know," I said impatiently. "Maybe she just spins around really fast and her costume appears or something."

"Or maybe she says some magic word and lightning strikes and that changes her into Ultraviolet!" Teddy offered.

"Don't you think we'd hear it if every time someone in this town was in trouble, lightning struck the teachers' lounge?" Fiona shot back.

"Guys!" I shouted. "It doesn't matter *how* she changes! It's just—let me finish! She opens her tote bag and pulls out a pair of boots, a purple cape, and a purple mask."

"We don't know for certain whether Ultraviolet wears a cape," Teddy reminded me.

"You know what I do know for certain?" Fiona added. "That Ms. Matthews carries her grade book in that tote bag. I've seen it, and I didn't see any purple boots in there."

"I told you I'm still working this out," I argued. "Just listen and stop interrupting."

They looked at each other and shrugged.

"She glances out the window to make sure she won't be spotted, and then she zips toward the screams at the speed of ultraviolet light. If anyone is watching, all he would see is a blur like the one I spotted last week. He can easily convince himself that his mind is playing tricks on him."

"Speaking of minds playing tricks . . . ," Fiona whispered loudly to Teddy.

I decided to ignore her.

"After Ms. Matthews saves the day, she streaks back toward the school at top speed," I continued. "She sails through the open window faster than the human eye can follow. Then she gets dressed and walks back to the classroom. All this takes less than a minute."

Teddy and Fiona shot each other sideways glances.

"What do you think?" I asked eagerly.

"It's a cool story, I guess," Teddy replied. "I think she should have a better exit than the window. And maybe she could have fought Painspider or—"

"It's not a story, Teddy!" I shouted in frustration. "I'm trying to explain to you guys how Ms. Matthews could transform into Ultraviolet even when she's at school."

"Okay, but don't you figure if she turns into Ultraviolet a couple times a day, she has to have more than one way to get in and out of the school without anyone seeing her?" Teddy argued. "If you were a superhero and you saw three kids standing outside the window of the room where you changed into your supercostume, wouldn't you go find another exit?"

"I can't believe I'm going to say this, but Teddy's right," Fiona agreed. "You have a theory, Nate, but you don't have any evidence. If you present what you just told us to Dr. Content, he's going to give you an F because you don't have anything to back it up."

"But Ms. Matthews knew that Ultraviolet wore a purple cape," I said. "The day after the bank robbery, she said everyone needed to get over their 'childish fantasy about flying women in purple capes saving the day.' Remember?"

They said nothing.

"We've seen every piece of news coverage about Ultraviolet," I said. "We've seen photos and videos, but we couldn't tell whether she was wearing a cape or a jacket or what her uniform really looked like. But Ms. Matthews knew. How could she possibly know unless it was *her own* costume?"

"She was *at* that bank robbery," Fiona pointed out. "She saw Ultraviolet, so she would have seen the cape."

"Then why didn't she say so on the news?" I demanded.

"She didn't care," Fiona sighed. "You know how she is about superheroes. Why would she care about what they wear enough to mention it on TV?"

"That's another good point," Teddy added. "She hates superheroes, so why would she be one?"

They made sense, but I knew in my gut that they were wrong and I was right. A gut feeling, however, is far from proof. Dr. Content had made that perfectly clear in his science class. I needed concrete evidence.

"There has to be a better way to prove it," Teddy said, trying to reassure me.

"There would be if there was anything to prove," Fiona grumbled.

"Fiona, Nate is our friend and we're sticking by him," Teddy said.

"Thanks, Teddy—" I started.

"It doesn't matter how stupid or crazy his ideas are," he continued. "We're a team. If he says Ms. Matthews is a superhero, we're going to waste as much time as it takes to prove him wrong." He patted me on the shoulder, but I hardly felt reassured.

"Fine," Fiona huffed. "But can we stop staring at this window and come up with a new plan tomorrow?"

We all agreed and started to walk home. Teddy was right. If Ms. Matthews was Ultraviolet, she'd know we were watching and just go change in the girls' bathroom or in the back of the cafeteria kitchen.

But when we reached the corner, I spun around quickly, just in case Ultraviolet was about to jump out the window and fly away.

No such luck.

I Am NOT Moping

When I got home, my sister was lounging on the couch with her shoes up on the coffee table, eating potato chips and watching *Cheery Happy Joy Penguin Squad.* Knowing she couldn't have already finished her homework, I counted at least three house rules she was breaking at once.

Normally, I would have snuck into the den, grabbed Dad's digital camera, and snapped some photographic evidence. I could then decide whether to e-mail them to him at work and get her in trouble immediately or save the pictures to use as blackmail the next time she caught me doing something I wasn't supposed to be doing. But I was so distracted I couldn't be bothered.

Instead, I plopped down on the couch beside Denise, settled my feet on the coffee table, and grabbed a handful of chips from the bag.

"Why are you watching this stupid show?" I asked with a groan.

"I like it," she muttered back without taking her eyes off the screen.

"It's for babies."

"No, it isn't," she countered. "Adults watch it in Japan. Don't blame me if you just can't appreciate international culture."

On the screen, a cartoon penguin danced in front of a flashing multicolored background while Japanese schoolchildren sang in a chorus. I shook my head.

Denise frowned. "What's wrong with you?"

"What makes you think there's anything wrong with me?" I asked.

"You haven't tried to grab the remote and change the channel yet, so it's obvious there's something distracting you."

Admitting to Denise that I was distracted because I was trying to prove that my history teacher was a superheroine was the last thing I wanted to do.

"It's nothing," I grunted as I stuffed some more chips into my mouth. "This baby show just hurts my eyes."

I could feel her staring at me, but I refused to make eye contact. She was trying to get a read on me, and I wasn't going to help her one bit.

"It's about Ultraviolet, isn't it?" she stated matter-of-factly.

"What?" I blurted, shifting uncomfortably on the couch and spitting some stray potato chip crumbs onto the coffee table. "Why would you think that?"

"For days, all you've talked about is Ultraviolet this and superhero that. Then, over the weekend, you stopped talking about her altogether and you got all . . . mopey."

"Mopey?"

"You moped all weekend."

"First off, I don't mope. Secondly, none of that means anything as far—"

She cut me off, holding her palm toward me dismissively and turning back to the TV. "Hang on, this is the best part."

The Cheery Happy Joy Penguin Squad marched in unison down a cobblestone path to the music of a synthesizer while a girl with huge eyes danced and leapt in elation behind them. If you'd offered me a million dollars to explain what made that "the best part" of the show, I wouldn't have been able to come even close.

The credits started to roll and Denise resumed her analysis. "I figure something happened with Ultraviolet. Since there haven't been any shocking new developments reported on the news, I'm guessing something happened just to you. Or maybe to you and your stupid friends?"

"Hey, my friends aren't—"

"Shhh, I'm thinking," she continued. "I'm guessing you must have seen her, but where? If she was at school, someone else would have seen her, too, and by now, everyone would be talking about it, so that can't be it."

She stared at me a little longer, deep in thought. "The only other place you go is the comic-book store, and if she went there, all you comic-nerd-heads would have exploded with excitement—"

"Hey, we're not nerd—"

"And I'd also expect if you saw her, you would be bragging, not moping."

"I am *not* moping," I insisted.

"Fine. Pouting," she suggested. "Maybe you saw her and she didn't live up to your expectations."

It was uncanny how close to the truth she was. Stupid Denise. I tried my best to keep a neutral look on my face. Suddenly, she snapped her fingers and pointed at me triumphantly. "You discovered her secret identity."

I choked on my potato chips.

"That's it!" Denise shouted. "Okay, who is she?"

I kept coughing and got up for a glass of water. Denise followed me.

"Does she work at the comic-book store?" she asked.

"Jeff is the only guy—*guy*—who works at the comic-book store," I reminded her between sips.

"Well, posing as a chubby, pasty-white, middle-aged guy who lives with his mom would be a pretty solid secret identity," she reasoned. "She could be a shape-shifter."

"Ultraviolet is *not* a shape-shifter. Zilch is the only hero with shape-shift—"

She smiled knowingly. "The fact that you are so insistent on that point while no one else—not even the police—is certain of her abilities tells me you have seen her out of costume and she was recognizable."

Sometimes it was just a bit annoying having a sister who was so smart. Other times, it was *extremely* annoying, and this was definitely one of those times.

Denise continued thinking aloud. "What females would be at the comic-book store? Is it Jeff's mom?"

I sighed. "Jeff's mom is in her seventies and never leaves the house!"

"Again, that would make for a really good secret identity," she said with a shrug. "Who would suspect a shut-in of being the most powerful superheroine in town?"

"It's *not* Jeff's mom," I said. "It's not anyone from the store."

She rolled her eyes skyward, as though seeking some inspiration from above. "That only leaves school," she whispered to herself. "The crossing guard? That would explain why she's always so distracted and doesn't help the elementary school kids when they want to cross the street. One of the lunch ladies would have plenty of free time to drop everything and rush off to rescue people."

She looked at me again and her eyes lit up. "Ms. Charlton, the gym teacher!" she shouted. "She's big and buff. I can totally see her beating up muggers and tossing around cars in her spare time."

To be honest, picturing Ms. Charlton doing those things didn't take much imagination.

"Look, I don't want to talk about it," I said.

"We're already talking about it," she persisted. "So tell me who Ultraviolet is."

"No, *you're* talking about it," I insisted. "I'm just listening to you babble about stuff that doesn't even make any sense." I was hoping to turn the tables on her.

"I think everything I'm saying makes perfect sense," Denise mused. "If it didn't, you wouldn't be acting the way you are. Now tell me Ultraviolet's secret identity."

I looked into her eyes and saw her determination. If I didn't tell her, she wasn't going to stop. I'd go to my grave with her incessant chatter ringing in my ears.

"It's Ms. Matthews," I said, relenting.

Denise nodded. I could see the wheels turning in her head as she pieced together stray facts and paired them with her own observations. Then a weird smile crept across her lips.

"You're crazy," she announced. "Ms. Matthews hates superheroes."

She picked up the remote, turned off the TV, and grabbed her backpack. As she walked up the stairs, I could hear her laughing at my expense.

Up, Up, and—Not That Way!

By lunch on Tuesday, I still hadn't come up with anything. Even with Teddy and Fiona pitching in, I had no way of proving that Ms. Matthews was, in fact, a superhero in disguise.

Teddy wanted to use our mental dead end as an excuse to ask Allison Heaton if she had any thoughts, but I quickly vetoed the idea.

"Why would you want to tell Allison Heaton?" I argued as I watched her and her friends on the opposite side of the cafeteria. "You know that girl can't keep a secret! If you ask her, by the end of the day, everyone will know I'm the crazy kid who thinks Ms. Matthews has superpowers."

"I'm not stupid enough to give her a name," he insisted as he took a big bite of his hoagie. "I'd just ask if she wanted to help us with your extra-credit project."

"But why Allison?" Fiona asked, though I had a hunch she already knew the answer. Teddy had had a crush on Allison, a tall, blond seventh grader, since he was in first grade and she was in second. When she was around, he had a tendency to boast to make himself seem cooler, and I could imagine he thought being hot on the trail of a superhero would be just the kind of thing that might make her remember that his name wasn't Ned, which was what she always called him.

"We've been trying to come up with a plan to prove your theory for two days now and haven't come up with anything," Teddy groaned. "Allison is the smartest girl in the school—"

"No, she's not," Fiona corrected sharply. "Just because she's smarter than you and you think she's pretty, that doesn't make her the smartest girl in the school."

Teddy tried to protest, but Fiona held up her hand to stop him.

"And just because you guys haven't come up with anything doesn't mean I haven't," she continued.

Teddy and I leaned in to hear what she had to say.

She lowered her voice and laid out her plan. "You're

never going to catch her here. She'll always be on her guard. You need to find her lair."

Any superhero worth anything has a lair of some sort so they can store their extra uniforms and equipment. It varies by hero and might be a cave, a penthouse suite, a tower, a warehouse by the docks, or a satellite in geosynchronous orbit twenty thousand miles above the Earth.

"That's a stupid plan," argued Teddy. "How are we going to do that? Type 'Ultraviolet's lair' into Google Maps?"

Fiona threw up her hands. "I don't know," she shot back. "Maybe we should ask Allison. No, I guess *that* would be stupid."

As they sniped at each other, I took a stack of comics from my backpack and laid them on the table. Fiona's plan wouldn't be easy, but it was the best idea we'd come up with. Looking over the comics, I noticed a running theme about the heroes and their headquarters.

"Stop fighting, guys," I interrupted. "Fiona's on to something, and I think I know how to find her base of operations."

Teddy shook his head. "How?"

I spread the comics in front of me. "Look at all these characters. Shiningstar and Astro have a secret room

ULTRAVIOLET
#1
SPECIAL ORIGIN ISSUE!!!
GUEST-STARRING
PHANTOM RANGER!!!

IT'S THE BIG, FLASHY STORIES OF WHERE SUPERPOWERS COME FROM THAT GET ALL THE ATTENTION.
SOMEONE GETS STRUCK BY LIGHTNING...
... OR VOLUNTEERS FOR A TOP SECRET GOVERNMENT EXPERIMENT...
... OR CRASHES TO THE EARTH FROM A DISTANT WORLD...
... AND A HERO IS BORN!
BUT FOR EVERY ONE OF THOSE STORIES, THERE ARE A LOT MORE THAT DON'T TURN OUT AS WELL.
TEST RESULTS: NEGATIVE
SORRY DUDE!
OXYGEN?
BUT- MY SPECIES... CAN'T...
...ACK!

TAKE IT FROM ME. MOST SUPERHEROES' ORIGINS ARE PRETTY BORING.
THE SECRET HISTORY OF ULTRAVIOLET
WRITTEN BY JAKE BELL
ILLUSTRATED BY CHRIS GIARRUSSO

USUALLY IT STARTS SIMPLY, LIKE WHEN YOU PICK UP SOMETHING HEAVIER THAN YOU THINK YOU COULD.
16 lbs
OTHER TIMES IT'S SOMETHING MORE OBVIOUS.
THE CHANGES MIGHT BE SUBTLE ENOUGH THAT NO ONE NOTICES.
IT'S BEEN SO LONG SINCE GRANNY'S SEEN YOU!
YOU'VE ALL GROWN SO MUCH!
YOU MIGHT NOT EVEN NOTICE YOURSELF.
LOOK AT YOU!
YOU'VE SHOT UP LIKE A WEED!
AND JUST AS YOU GET USED TO THE IDEA OF HAVING SUPERPOWERS...
YOU OKAY OVER THERE, PUMPKIN?
I'M FINE, DAD.
TAKE YOUR TIME.

...YOU FIND MAYBE YOU DON'T WANT THEM AFTER ALL.
HOMECOMING GAME 2:00PM SATURDAY
...HIGH FIVE AFTER A GOOD PLAY, SHE MIGHT BREAK YOUR HAND.
...MESS HER HAIR UP FLYING TO SCHOOL...
NO WAY! YOU INVITE HER!
JUST IMAGINE THE SUPER GERMS SHE MIGHT...
MAYBE SHE SHOULD BE PLAYING LINEBACKER...
I JUST WANT TO BE A NORMAL KID LIKE EVERYONE ELSE!
I DON'T WANT TO HAVE SUPERPOWERS!
SOB!
SO I TRANSFERRED TO A NEW SCHOOL ON THE OTHER SIDE OF TOWN WHERE I COULD BE A NEW ME.
MY FAMILY JUST MOVED HERE FROM CANADA, SO I DON'T KNOW ANYONE AROUND HERE.
UM... EH?

UNFORTUNATELY, IT'S NOT ALWAYS EASY TO PRETEND YOU DON'T HAVE SUPERPOWERS.
DARWYN CITY.
AT LAST I HAVE YOU, PHANTOM RANGER! THERE IS NO ESCAPE!
DON'T BE SO CERTAIN, TERRORANTULA!
KRRSSHH!

THANKS FOR THE ASSIST BACK THERE.
THAT WAS QUICK THINKING.
HAVE YOU EVER GIVEN ANY THOUGHT TO BEING A SUPERHERO?
I DON'T KNOW WHAT YOU'RE TALKING ABOUT.
I'M TALKING ABOUT SUPER STRENGTH ENHANCED SPEED, A LEVEL OF INVULNERABILITY, AND--IF I'M NOT MISTAKEN--FLIGHT ABILITY.
I'M-- I'M NOT INTERESTED IN... YOU KNOW.
IN BEING A SUPERHERO? YEAH, SO I'VE GATHERED.
I'VE BEEN WAITING A LONG TIME TO TALK TO YOU ABOUT THIS.
YOU MUST HAVE ME CONFUSED WITH SOMEONE ELSE.
I'M NOT FROM AROUND HERE--
NO, YOU'RE FROM KANIGHER FALLS, RIGHT?
THE THING IS, WE DON'T HAVE A SUPERHERO IN KANIGHER FALLS RIGHT NOW, AND I HAVE REASON TO BELIEVE WE'RE GOING TO NEED ONE THERE SOON.
I MAY NOT HAVE WANTED TO BE A SUPERHERO, BUT EVEN I KNEW THAT WHEN PHANTOM RANGER ASKED YOU FOR A FAVOR, YOU DIDN'T SAY NO.

KANIGHER FALLS, TWO DAYS LATER...
BEAN THERE DONE THAT
FUNNY PAGES
COMICS GAMES TOYS CARDS
I TOLD THE DESIGNER YOU LIKE PURPLE. THIS IS WHAT SHE CAME UP WITH.
I WAS EVEN THINKING YOU COULD USE PURPLE IN YOUR NAME.
AREN'T WE GETTING A LITTLE AHEAD OF OURSELVES? DON'T I GET SOME KIND OF TRAINING?
I'M WORKING ON IT. IN THE MEANTIME, GO WITH YOUR INSTINCTS.
LIKE WITH THE CHUNK OF CEMENT.
NOW, WHAT DO YOU THINK OF PURPLE GIRL?
I REALLY DON'T FEEL COMFORTABLE WITH PUTTING ON A COSTUME AND FLYING AROUND TOWN WITHOUT SOME KIND OF CLASS OR A MANUAL--
I ASSURE YOU, WE'LL GET YOU TRAINING.
BUT FIRST WE HAVE TO GET YOU NOTICED...
...AS PRINCESS PURPLE?
SUPER PURPLE?
POWER PURPLE?
LILAC LIGHTNING?
INDIGO EMPRESS?
HOW ABOUT ULTRAVIOLET?
COMICS GAMES TOYS CARDS
HA HA, YES!
ULTRAVIOLET!
THAT'S PERFECT!
I GUESS.
I MEAN, THIS IS ONLY TEMPORARY, RIGHT?
DID YOU SEE THAT NEW CAMERAPHONE VIDEO OF PHANTOM RANGER FIGHTING TERRORANTULA ON YOUTUBE?
IT MAY NOT BE FLASHY, IT MAY NOT BE EXCITING, BUT THAT'S HOW I BECAME ULTRAVIOLET.

under their garage. Nightowl operates out of his attic. Serpentina has a giant snake cave under her house and—"

"I'm not following you," Fiona interrupted.

"The most convenient place to keep your stuff if you're a superhero would be in your house, or at least near your house," I explained.

"Hammer and Sickle's fortress is in the Siberian tundra," Fiona argued. "The Hurricane Squad headquarters is on the moon."

"True," I acknowledged. "But those comics are about heroes who work all over the world. Ultraviolet has only been seen in Kanigher Falls. It wouldn't make sense for her to have to fly up to the moon every time she has to change into her costume."

"Whirlwolf maintains a series of storage lockers throughout the city—" Teddy pointed out.

I cut him off. "Do you have a better idea?"

The only answer he had was to pick up the issue of *Nightowl* from the table and start reading.

"I didn't think so," I said.

"Even if you're right, we don't know where Ms. Matthews lives," Fiona said.

"That's what we need to find out," I agreed. "We'll follow her home after school."

Fiona leaned back in her chair, her brow creased in a frown. "Count me out! I'm not stalking someone who decides whether or not we move on to seventh grade next year."

She had a good point. "I guess you're right. We can't risk getting caught, and shadowing someone who could have supersensitive hearing and vision won't be easy."

Teddy looked up from the comic with a broad smile. "Leave that to me."

o o o

Later that afternoon, Teddy led me and Fiona to the basketball courts next to the faculty parking lot.

"What are we doing?" Fiona asked.

"We're going to wait for her over here," Teddy explained. "When she leaves, we'll track her."

"And how do we do that?" Fiona demanded.

Teddy handed her the copy of *Nightowl* he'd read at lunch. "Check it out."

As we reached the courts, Fiona skimmed the comic, trying to figure out what Teddy had in mind.

Sometimes hiding isn't about finding something big to get behind or wearing camouflage and jumping into the bushes. Sometimes you can hide right out in the open, like three kids standing in a crowd of other kids playing basketball. I had to hand it to Teddy: This wasn't a bad idea. No one would spot us as long as—

"See you tomorrow, guys!" Ms. Matthews shouted. I looked toward the parking lot and saw her walking to her car, waving to us. "Don't forget to study for your quiz on the Harlem Renaissance."

I waved back and smiled, disappointed. I wondered how long it would take us to devise a Plan B. Teddy waved too, but then leaned over to whisper to us, "Okay, let's go."

"Go?" I asked. "But she saw—"

Teddy took off toward the gym as fast as he could. I grabbed Fiona by the arm and towed her after him.

He stopped at a maintenance access ladder bolted to the side of the building. The janitor used it when the air conditioner broke or Meathead threw some kid's backpack onto the roof. A metal cage covered the bottom six feet of the ladder and was padlocked shut, but Teddy was able to scale it without much trouble.

"What are you doing?" I shouted after him.

"Hurry," he urged, waving me upward.

I scrambled around the metal cage to grasp the first exposed rung of the ladder. Then I pulled myself to the top of the three-story building. Fiona was close behind me.

As I crawled onto the roof, I saw Teddy on the far side, crouching and looking over the edge. When I walked up beside him, he thrust his finger toward the street, pointing out Ms. Matthews's car as she waited to pull into traffic.

"Do you want to explain your plan to us yet?" I urged.

"Did you read the comic?" he asked.

Fiona took the book from her back pocket, which was where she'd crammed it so she could climb the ladder. I gasped in horror as she unfolded what once had been a pristine copy. "I've looked, but I don't know what you're talking about."

Teddy snatched it away, crumpling the pages further. He opened it to the middle and handed it to me. On the page, Nightowl was crouched on a rooftop, looking down. I couldn't help noticing the similarity to Teddy's pose.

I read aloud from the comic: "'Fools! They take so many precautions to make sure they aren't being followed, but they never look up.'"

In the next panel, Nightowl dove from the edge of the roof to a gargoyle perched on the next building over. Then he shot a grappling hook to another overhang and swung to his third landing, continuing this way until he arrived at the bad guys' hideout. Fiona grabbed the comic to see for herself.

Ms. Matthews's car lurched forward and pulled away from the school.

"I don't—what are you thinking, Teddy?" I asked.

"You were worried she might see us, but she'll never think to look up."

I peered over the eave to see the closest rooftop, which was at least fifteen feet away and twenty feet down. Even if we were stupid enough to make the jump and somehow succeeded without breaking our legs, the next building from there was clear on the other side of the soccer field. I looked at Fiona. She shrugged.

"Are you telling us you were planning to pursue her across the rooftops?" I asked.

"She'll never see us coming," he said smugly.

"What rooftops, Teddy?"

Teddy looked around in disbelief, as though this was the first time he'd even bothered to notice where we were.

"Yeah, it's not like we're atop a skyscraper amidst an urban jungle of concrete and glass," Fiona commented drily.

Teddy and I both gave her a look.

"What?" she asked, holding up the *Nightowl* comic.

"It's right here." She read aloud: "'Perched atop a skyscraper amidst an urban jungle of concrete and glass, Nightowl watches and listens, waiting for his next opportunity to fight crime in whatever form it takes.'"

Teddy lowered his head in embarrassment. "Sorry, guys, I . . ."

I let out a groan of frustration as I watched Ms. Matthews's car disappear down the road. Fiona laughed and hit Teddy with the comic book. Normally, I would have cared about her damaging it, but I was too focused on watching our plan—our terrible, terrible plan—go down the toilet.

Then, as quickly as it had vanished, hope reappeared.

About half a mile down the road, Ms. Matthews changed lanes and turned left onto Swan Drive. I finally knew how I was going to track her.

What Lunch Money? I Packed My Lunch

The next morning, I rode my bike to school. I told Teddy that I had to get home extra fast that afternoon because I had a dentist appointment. I didn't like lying to him, but I couldn't risk having him screw up my new plan for tracking Ms. Matthews.

While I locked up my bike, I spotted Dr. Content carrying a stack of circuit boards and other components that looked like they'd come from a few dozen gutted computers.

"Need some help, Mr. Content?" I offered.

"Doctor. It's *Doctor* Content, Nate—and yes, I could use an extra hand, thanks."

We took the computer parts to his classroom. He unlocked the class laboratory and put everything we'd carried onto a table.

"What are these things?" I asked.

"Oh, microprocessors and monitoring systems and . . . stuff. How's that extra-credit project coming along?"

"Great," I lied. "Lots of good . . . um, data and observational . . . stuff."

Dr. Content looked skeptical. "Mind if I take a look at your data and 'observational stuff'?"

"Well, I don't really have anything with me right now. . . ."

"Nate, I'm not going to accuse you of lying, because that would be rude," he said gently. "However, I have reason to suspect maybe you haven't collected as much data as you let on. Is that fair to say?"

I nodded.

Dr. Content let out a sigh and leaned toward me. "Nate, I know doing extra work isn't much fun. You have classmates who have an easy time getting good grades. And I'm sure you look at them and wonder what they did to deserve such a simple life while you have to work and fight for everything."

I nodded again.

"You can't judge yourself against someone else's lucky breaks, though," he continued. "There will always be someone smarter or better-looking or more popular"—he smiled and rubbed his hand across the top of his bald head—"or with more hair. You can only worry about what you have and whether you're making the most of it. The problem here, Nate, is that you're not making the most of your talents."

I took a deep breath and looked away.

"I want to see you work hard on this project, but if you're not interested, just say so now—"

"I'm interested!" I insisted. "I've just hit a few dead ends."

"Just keep at it, Mr. Banks," he said. "I look forward to your next progress report."

ooo

When classes let out, I rode up to Swan Drive, parked beside a field where some kids were playing flag football, and sat with my back to a tree. From my vantage point, I could see a stretch of road almost a mile long. There was no way I was going to miss her.

Ms. Matthews had to live either on this street or on one of the others that branched off from it. All I had to do was wait until her car turned onto Swan, then observe where she turned and go investigate. It wouldn't be long before I uncovered Ultraviolet's secret fortress, earned myself an A in science, and convinced my friends I wasn't crazy.

That is, unless Fiona was right and Ultraviolet's secret fortress *was* on the moon. I still didn't know what I was going to do in that case.

Of course, I had plenty of time to think about it, but no ideas came leaping to mind. So I opened my backpack, took out some comic books, and got some important reading out of the way.

I was deeply engrossed in the latest issue of *Spin Doctors*—in which President Hornsby's new chief of staff is revealed to be the Weasel—when my patience was finally rewarded. Ms. Matthews's green sedan turned onto the road about a quarter of a mile away. I carefully placed the comics back into my bag and slipped behind the tree for cover.

Then I felt a tap on my shoulder.

Startled, I spun around to face Meathead McCaskill.

"Hey, Banks," he growled. "Whatcha doin'?"

"Oh, hi, Meat—I mean, Ang—um . . . Hey, man," I stammered. "Not much." I tried to turn back to the street, but Meathead grabbed my shoulder and spun me to face him again.

"Where's your lunch money, Banks?"

"I packed my lunch," I said. "Even if I hadn't, I would have spent it already. Lunchtime was four hours ago."

"Oh." He paused. "What about tomorrow's lunch money?"

"Well, I'm going to pack my lunch again. But even if I was going to bring some lunch money, I wouldn't have it yet," I explained while I glanced at the street. Ms. Matthews was passing us now and I made an effort to keep an eye on her, but Meathead wouldn't let that happen.

"Hey, look at me when I'm talking to you!" he snarled as he grabbed my face and twisted it back toward his own.

"I just told you I don't have any lunch mon—" I was cut short when Meathead buried his fist in my stomach. I dropped to my knees on the grass, trying to breathe. While I was down, he grabbed my wallet from my pocket and took out the three dollars I'd been saving for my weekly comic-store visit.

Meathead crumpled up the bills and shoved them into his pocket. Then he threw my wallet to the ground and took off down the street.

I scrambled to my feet to see if I could still catch Ms. Matthews, though I knew it was pointless. Someone *pushing* a car could have made it to her destination by the time I flopped over to the curb to look down the street. As I'd figured, Ms. Matthews's car was nowhere to be seen.

I rubbed my stomach and groaned as I grabbed my bike and headed home. There had to be an easier way to do this.

Um...Vote for Nate?

Usually I looked forward to Thursday. Thursday meant that the school week was nearly over, and it was all downhill to the weekend. All the comic blogs had reviews of the new batch of comics on Thursdays, giving me a list of what to buy on Friday. And to top it all off, Thursday was Pizza Day in the cafeteria.

But what made Thursday great could also make it awful. Knowing that the weekend was approaching, some teachers sensed they were behind schedule and tried to cram in an extra lesson or double up the homework. I was facing the same type of problem. If I didn't figure out a new plan to unveil Ms. Matthews's secret identity soon, I'd have to wait through the entire weekend to try again. I couldn't stake out Swan Drive again. Meathead would be looking for me. I needed to find a new way of tracking her, but I was fresh out of ideas.

In history class, I watched Ms. Matthews as she wrote on the chalkboard and pointed to the map mounted to the wall. She hid her alter ego well. She certainly didn't move like someone with superpowers, and her voice hardly had the commanding tone you would expect from someone I suspected could bench-press a steamroller.

As she wrapped up class, Ms. Matthews pushed her glasses up the bridge of her nose and cleared her throat.

"I'm certain you all heard this during the morning announcements, but I thought I would remind you that the elections for student council will be held one week from today. As the student council sponsor, I'll be submitting the list of candidates. So if you or anyone you know would like to run for office, please let me know by the end of the day."

I paid no attention at first. After all, running for office meant giving a speech in front of the whole school.

"If you have any questions, I'll be available after class," she continued. "I'll also be happy to advise anyone who needs help putting together a campaign."

As she finished her sentence, the bell rang. Everyone leapt from their seats and raced to the door. Ms. Matthews watched them go. When she turned back, she seemed surprised to see me.

"Yes, Nathan?" she asked.

I braced myself, already imagining the eyes of the entire school staring at me as I made my campaign speech. But working closely with Ms. Matthews to put together a campaign would give me the perfect excuse to remain close to her.

"Where do I sign up?" I squeaked.

o o o

Mom walked in from the garage, looking like she'd been run over by two buses. Sadly, that was an improvement over many days. The hospital was understaffed, and lately she'd been working about sixty hours a week.

"What's for dinner?" she rasped tiredly, lifting the lid from the pot on the stove. "Macaroni and cheese with chopped hot dogs?" Her shoulders slumped even further. "My favorite." She sighed.

Unfortunately, with my dad working late hours—he was an accountant and his company was going through a huge merger—Mom had little choice but to accept what Denise had made us an hour earlier and left to get cold on the stove. She scraped a glutinous glob of yellow mush speckled with little chunks of pink into a bowl and microwaved it for thirty seconds.

I approached slowly. When Mom was this tired, it was best not to startle her with any sudden movements or loud noises. "Mom?"

She turned and smiled, putting an arm around my shoulder and pulling me closer to kiss the top of my head. "Hey, kiddo," she greeted me. "How was school?"

The microwave beeped and she withdrew the bowl. She grabbed a can of soda from the fridge, kicked the door closed, and sat down at the table. I sat in the chair on the other side and slid a piece of paper from school across the table.

With her mouth still full of her first bite of hot dog mac and cheese, she dropped her fork. "What did you do now, Nate? Did you fail another test? Not do your homework?"

"No, I—"

"I'm too tired for this, Nate," she insisted, resting her elbows on the table and pressing her eyes with the heels of her hands. "I'm working too much, as always. Your dad didn't get home until after ten last night, and then he was up doing paperwork until one in the morning. Can you just stay out of trouble for a few weeks? Is that so much—"

"Mom!" I interjected. "I didn't do anything wrong! This is a permission slip saying you're okay with letting me run for student council."

She sat up straight and took her hands from her eyes, which were red and heavy. She smiled, taking the form. "Student council? What are you runn—oh, vice president?"

I had decided on vice president by default. I knew there was no way I wanted to be president, and I was terrible at math, so treasurer was out. That left secretary and vice president. Most days, my handwriting was barely legible, so vice president won.

"Did I ever tell you about the time I ran for student council treasurer when I was in sixth grade?" Mom asked eagerly. She had been on the student council in elementary school, middle school, and high school, and she had told me all about her sixth-grade elections. Several times. But that didn't stop her from telling me again. She'd lost to a kid named Mickey Bishop, who had passed out buttons with a close-up photo of a finger stuck up a nose and the slogan "Pick Mick!"

"That afternoon was the second time I met Phantom Ranger," she recalled. "My best friend, Carrie, and I got out of school and he was on patrol. When we got to the crosswalk, he landed beside us and asked, 'How was school today, girls?' but I was in no mood to talk."

I'd heard the story countless times, and with every telling, my mom puffed out her chest and did the same booming-voice impersonation for Phantom Ranger.

"He looked right at me and asked what was wrong.

Carrie told him I'd lost the election. He put his hand on my shoulder and said, 'It's okay, Paige. If you don't give up, I bet you'll win next year.'"

Of course, just that Phantom Ranger knew my mom's name served as an inferred endorsement, and she was elected student body president in a landslide the following year.

"So what kind of strategy are you going to use?" she asked. "What are the important issues you want to address?" My mother, who had seemed half dead only minutes before, was positively hyperactive. "Have you thought of any slogans?"

"Um . . . 'Vote for Nate'?" I proposed.

Her smile faded. She looked down at the mound of yellow in front of her.

"Did you eat this?"

"A little bit, yeah."

"Why don't you order a pizza? I'll get changed, and we'll work on your campaign strategy."

I didn't have the heart to tell her I didn't really want to win and was only running to prove my teacher was a superhero. Plus I was seriously in the mood for some pizza. So I nodded and grabbed the phone.

Glitter Never Washes Off

Dr. Content studied the three pages of notes I'd scribbled on loose-leaf paper. "This is very good work, Nate," he said as he handed the papers back to me. "I'm fascinated to see where this goes."

"I don't want to jinx anything—" I began, but he held up a hand to stop me.

"Jinxes are superstition, not science," he insisted. "Do you have a hypothesis you wish to prove?"

I bit my lip for a second and grinned. "I think I may have discovered Ultraviolet's secret identity."

"Really?" he whispered, his eyes sparkling with excitement.

"I . . . Well, at this point, I don't have any hard evidence," I admitted.

"I understand. But who do you think she is?"

Dr. Content was one of the few people who treated me

like an intelligent human being and didn't look down on me because I liked comic books. I worried that telling him that I thought one of his coworkers was a superhero might change his opinion of me.

"I probably shouldn't say until I've gathered some more data," I said. "You keep telling us about the scientific method and all."

Dr. Content looked a little disappointed.

"Absolutely," he agreed. "You'll have to forgive me. I'm just excited, as I'm sure you are as well. You're right, though. When we find a theory we want to be true, we are more likely to ignore contrary evidence and embrace supporting evidence."

He put his fingers together like a tent in front of his lips.

"Before I got laid off from the power plant, I had a long-standing argument with some of my colleagues on that very topic. So as much as I'd love to know who you think is walking around town with purple and white Spandex underneath her clothes, I will be"—he paused and smiled, searching for the right word—"patient."

"Well, the project is due in a week and a half, so you shouldn't have to wait too long," I pointed out. "I plan to do some intense observation of my subject in that time."

"Excellent, Mr. Banks," he said. "I look forward to your findings!"

o o o

That afternoon and throughout the entire following week, I spent more time in Ms. Matthews's classroom than I ever could have imagined. Before school, during lunch, after school—I sat at my desk, allegedly plotting a campaign strategy based on my mother's suggestions. But truly I was wondering whether I would throw up on the podium during my speech.

Of course, the entire reason I was there was to see if Ms. Matthews would excuse herself to go save a sinking ocean liner or divert a meteor headed straight for city hall. Unfortunately, I wasn't able to keep as close a watch as I'd originally hoped.

Every few minutes, she excused herself. She'd go to meetings with the other history teachers or pick up some papers in the office or run off copies of a handout for the next day's lesson. But when she left, I had no idea if she was really going where she said she was or if it was just a ruse to cover that she was off to catch a news helicopter that ran out of fuel and was going to crash into an orphanage.

On top of that, I'd watch the news every night and read

the paper every day to track Ultraviolet sightings and try to match them up with times when Ms. Matthews might have been out of sight.

On Tuesday, a stolen sarcophagus was returned to the Historical Society Museum, and the thieves were found tied up on the front steps. Everyone suspected that Ultraviolet had been involved. Could this have happened while I was trying to find a word to rhyme with "Nate" for my campaign buttons? Or maybe it had happened while Teddy was busy rolling dried rubber cement into fake boogers and sticking them to my face.

Try as I might to keep tabs on her various comings and goings, I'd find myself so bogged down making campaign posters that half the time I didn't even notice her leaving the room. I'd managed to convince Teddy and Fiona to help me, but mostly they just distracted me from monitoring Ms. Matthews.

"How many of these signs do we really need?" Teddy complained as he laid another sheet of poster board across the long table at the back of the room.

"I don't know," I said with a shrug. "A hundred?"

Teddy looked at the pile of completed signs and then looked back at me. "We've been here for an hour and we've only made nine."

Fiona wasn't helping at all. She sat at the end of the table, hunched over a comic book. Her assistance was limited to handing me markers that had rolled out of my reach, and even that was done with a huff of frustration.

Worse yet, my official report for Dr. Content was still heavy on speculation, which I knew wouldn't make him happy. He might have been impressed with the initial theories I'd shown him, but ultimately he wanted facts, and all I had was some circumstantial evidence. It was clear I couldn't just sit around waiting for proof to fall into my lap. I had to devise a way of forcing Ms. Matthews to reveal her superpowers. But with every hour of breathing in the fumes of markers and rubber cement from the stacks of campaign posters, I was coming up with fewer ideas, not more.

How do you fool someone into accidentally showing off her superstrength? Do you drop your keys under a school bus and hope she lifts it before she notices what she's doing? Hire a crane to drop a steel girder on the roof of the school?

But what could I really prove? I'd almost been snapped into three pieces by the Ditko Middle School football team, and that hadn't convinced anyone of anything.

I could launch two nuclear missiles at opposite coasts

to see if she could stop them both. Or I could build a weaponized suit of armor and attack the school.

The more I pondered, the more my plans sounded like the insane plots of either a supervillain or my best friend, Teddy.

o o o

On Tuesday afternoon, I was standing on a stepladder, getting ready to tape a banner outside the school's office, when Ms. Matthews walked by. Her eyes darted from side to side suspiciously, as if she was trying to determine whether anyone was watching her. Then she ducked into a supply closet.

"Be careful up there," Teddy grumbled as he hoisted the banner over his head. "If you fall, you'd better not land on me."

"Huh?" I muttered. I glanced from the supply closet door to Teddy. I wondered if Ms. Matthews was donning purple boots and a cape inside—and if she could somehow use the air-conditioning vents to exit the school through the roof.

"I said hurry up," he groaned. "My arms are falling asleep."

"Sorry," I replied. I took the banner and tried to anchor the center with a piece of tape that just wouldn't stick to the chalky tiles.

"Look at this," Teddy complained. "I've got glitter all over my hands from this stupid thing. Aw, it's on my shirt, too. Why did you use so much glitter?"

"I don't know," I said with a shrug. "Ms. Matthews gave me glitter. I used it."

"I think it sends the wrong message to the electorate," Teddy said.

"Huh?" I asked, still distracted by Ms. Matthews's trip to the supply room.

"You heard me—the el-ec-tor-ate," Teddy repeated slowly. "Some of us pay attention during history class."

As I pushed my thumb against the tape, he railed on.

"You know, glitter never washes off," he complained. "I'll still have glitter on this shirt two months from now."

Ms. Matthews still hadn't emerged from the supply closet. I could sense that this might be my one and only chance to prove my theory. If I threw open the door and she was gone, I'd finally have my undeniable evidence.

Quickly, I stuck a piece of tape on the last corner and pressed it against the wall—too quickly, in fact. The shift in my weight threw the ladder off balance. Teddy was busy examining his shirt, and he didn't grab and steady the ladder fast enough. In an attempt to steady it as it tipped toward him, he threw his shoulder into the side of the ladder, knocking it out from under me.

The ladder was going one way and I was going the other. I was headed straight for my best friend, who at this point was looking more like a landing pad. I fell on top of him, driving us both into the floor.

Meanwhile, the metal ladder smashed into the drinking fountain, making a horrendous noise. The clattering of aluminum against steel brought Principal Gwynn running from his office. Judging from his expression, I could only assume he had been expecting to see a stray bulldozer that had driven through the wall instead of two groaning kids in a tangled pile on the floor.

"What happened here?" he demanded.

"I was hanging my campaign banner," I muttered.

"Get off me," Teddy moaned.

Principal Gwynn helped me to my feet and then offered a hand to Teddy.

"Boys, you need to be more careful," he scolded us.

"Sorry," I wheezed. "I guess I just got distracted."

At that moment, the door to the supply closet opened and Ms. Matthews emerged. She took one step, then stopped to stare at us, apparently not sure what to make of the scene.

"What were you doing in there?" I blurted out accusingly.

"And where were you twenty seconds ago?" Teddy grumbled under his breath. "Some superhero you are."

"I was getting staples," she explained as she held up a box. "I'm sure you noticed my stapler was empty before you went to hang that banner."

"Why would I have noticed that?" I asked.

"If you're going to hang banners on those tile walls, you have to staple them to the staple strip," she said matter-of-factly. "Tape won't stick."

As if on cue, the tape pulled away from the wall, dropping the banner on top of Principal Gwynn, Teddy, and me. Principal Gwynn pushed it away, looking at his hand and his suit coat.

"Glitter, Nate?" He shook his head. "You know, this stuff never washes off."

I DO Want to Be a Superhero

By Thursday, I still hadn't found one piece of concrete evidence. On Wednesday, Ultraviolet had caught a three-ton freight container that had broken loose from a crane cable down in the warehouse district, saved eight people from a fire in a restaurant, and returned an escaped orangutan to the zoo, but there was no way I could tie any of that to Ms. Matthews.

And I still had to get up in front of the entire school to make a campaign speech for a position I didn't want. There was a very serious risk that when my name was announced, the audience would laugh me off the stage. Everyone at school knew me as the nerdy kid who loved superheroes. Fiona could barely muster the support to help make a campaign poster, and Teddy had written off my "stupid crusade" after the ladder incident.

"If she was a superhero, don't you think she would have saved us?" he'd argued with me on the way home.

"Not necessarily," I said. "It's not like our lives were in danger. She weighed our safety against the secrecy of her identity—"

"Stop it, Nate," he interrupted. "You know you're my best friend, but this has gone far enough."

If my best friends didn't believe in me, what chance was there that anyone else would? And the more I thought about it, the more I was kind of hoping I *would* be laughed off the stage. It would get me out of making my speech.

Right after homeroom on Thursday morning, all the candidates had to meet in the music room. Principal Gwynn gave us a little pep talk, explaining the importance of student council officers and reminding us that regardless of the outcome, we all were winners in his book. I spent the majority of his talk drying my sweaty palms on my legs and then worrying that I would have long streaks of sweat staining my pants by the time I went onstage. This, of course, made my palms sweat even more.

While Principal Gwynn talked, Ms. Matthews graded some papers in the corner. When he finished, she stood up and reminded us of the order in which we'd give our speeches. As she spoke, I couldn't help thinking that maybe Teddy and Fiona were right. My plot to find evidence tying her to Ultraviolet had failed to turn up anything, despite days of constant surveillance. Worse, it had made me out to be a madman and had taken me away from my closest friends.

Now I was minutes away from walking to the podium. I would rather have been walking to the gallows.

"Okay, let's go," Ms. Matthews said briskly.

She tapped her papers on a music stand to straighten them. Almost immediately, her hand recoiled and she inhaled sharply, sticking the tip of her index finger into her mouth.

"Yeesh!" she exclaimed. "Paper cut."

My eyes widened. As I watched Ms. Matthews shake her hand vigorously, I realized I'd finally gotten the evidence I'd been searching for.

According to every news story I'd read, Ultraviolet seemed capable of stopping bullets with her outstretched palms. I assumed she would barely register the point of a mugger's knife before the blade snapped off against her skin. Nothing seemed to hurt her no matter what the bad guys might try. It wouldn't surprise me if Ultraviolet could survive a nuclear blast without so much as a scratch. I had a pretty good hunch that she was also immune to paper cuts.

Stunned, I barely heard her tell us to make our way out to the auditorium. I followed Dustin Hobson, who was running for treasurer, and sat next to him on the stage. One by one, the candidates gave their speeches.

Still dazed by the backstage revelation, I didn't notice when it was my turn.

"Nate!" Principal Gwynn whisper-shouted from the opposite side of the stage. I turned my head in his direction to see him pointing vigorously at the podium.

"It's your turn," he mouthed.

My throat went dry and my eyes went blurry as I looked out at the student body. Weakly, I smiled and got to my feet. With every step, my shoes felt like they each weighed about thirty pounds.

When I finally reached the podium, I realized that the speech my mom had helped me write was crumpled in my fist, damp with sweat. I smoothed it out as best as I could while I chewed nervously on my lower lip.

"MynameisNateBanks," I read quickly, running my words together. "And I want to be" — I paused and pointed my finger aimlessly at random audience members — "*your* student body vice president."

I looked up from my paper and scanned the crowd, a

lump clogging my throat. I tried to swallow but couldn't. Then my eyes fell on Ms. Matthews in the front row. She smiled and motioned for me to keep talking with a wave of her hand. I could see a yellow bandage on her finger.

I pushed my speech aside and leaned toward the microphone. I'd been thinking about something for weeks but only now realized what it was. Something came over me, and I suddenly felt I had to get it off my chest.

"You guys know me as the kid who talks about superheroes all the time, right?"

The crowd didn't give me much of a reply.

"And most of you think I'm a little *too* crazy about superheroes, right? Most of you probably think that I want to *be* a superhero, right?"

Now I had a few heads nodding.

"A few weeks ago, I convinced myself that I'd figured out Ultraviolet's true identity. I've spent more time than I'd like to admit trying to . . . catch her."

I could hear muffled laughter, but I continued anyway.

"What I've realized now is how much time I wasted. I wasted time trying to spot Ultraviolet. I wasted time trying to learn her identity. And it was a waste because it doesn't matter who she is. It only matters what she does.

"Sure, superheroes are great, because they can do amazing things to help people who can't help themselves. They can stop bank robbers or rush into burning buildings and save people's lives.

"Superheroes do those great things for us, but we can't just sit around waiting for them to fix all our problems. Sometimes we have to be superheroes ourselves. If being a superhero means helping someone with something that he can't do for himself, we all have that power."

I could tell that the crowd was really listening now.

"As your vice president, I *do* want to be a superhero . . . and I want all of you to be superheroes, too," I continued. I wasn't sure if I sounded cheesy or inspired, but I was already too deep to change course. "I want to solve problems and help my classmates and I want to attend a school where everyone looks out for one another. Thank you."

I turned to go back to my seat as the audience applauded. I couldn't really hear it myself, but Fiona assured me later that it had been genuine.

Regardless, the election was a landslide, and it wasn't in my favor. I know I got my own vote, and Fiona assured me she marked my name on her ballot. Teddy swore he voted for me, but he'd been too excited about getting to tell Allison Heaton, who'd been elected seventh-grade president, that he was my campaign manager to remember whether he had turned in his ballot. I got about twenty other people to put down my name, too, but that was it.

Despite the outcome, I felt pretty good about the day. Not only had I faced my fear of public speaking head-on, but I'd relieved myself of the burden of proving that my teacher was a superhero by proving she wasn't. Plus the week was almost over, and Teddy, Fiona, and I were already certain of what new comics we'd be buying the following day.

"There's a new issue of *Whirlwolf* out." Teddy bubbled with excitement as we walked home. "I read on the Internet that Mr. Enigma is going to reveal Whirlwolf's secret identity to a reporter from the *Tribune*."

"That's no big deal," I said. "That just means in two or three issues he'll find some other superhero to put on the Whirlwolf costume so they can be seen at the same time."

"They did that last year in *Sisteroid*," Fiona said. Teddy and I just shrugged.

"Only girls read *Sisteroid*," Teddy muttered.

Fiona protested, "Hey, *Sisteroid* is a good—" But her defense was cut short by the squealing of truck tires.

The crossing guard had just stepped into the street

to let some of the elementary school kids cross. As I spun to look at the huge truck skidding toward the crosswalk, it was clear it wasn't going to stop in time. Some kids scrambled toward the curb, but two little kids stood perfectly still, frozen with a look of horror on their faces.

The crossing guard didn't see them as she rushed to get out of the way. When the truck hit, I closed my eyes and turned away, and all I heard was the sound of breaking glass and twisting metal. When I opened my eyes, I couldn't believe what I saw.

The two kids were still standing in the middle of the crosswalk, completely unharmed. The front end of the truck was smashed to pieces, like a china platter dropped on a tile floor. The entire engine was twisted and had caved in on itself, forming a cocoon of safety around the kids.

Ultraviolet stepped out from the middle of the steel cocoon. In the split second it had taken me to close my eyes, she had swooped down from the sky and planted herself between the truck and the students, absorbing the force of several tons of speeding metal without flinching. She carefully led the two kids to the safety of the sidewalk while the rest of us stared in shock.

She wore purple shorts, but with her matching cape

behind her, I could see how some eyewitnesses might mistake them for a skirt. Her most interesting feature was a pair of white goggles with purple lenses. No one had mentioned those after any of the previous sightings. I'd always just assumed she wore a mask.

With the kids safe, Ultraviolet turned her attention to the driver, who was still sitting in the cab of the truck. Effortlessly, she tore the door from its hinges and dropped it to the street. Then she scooped up the man behind the wheel and flew off in the direction of the hospital in a streak of purple and white.

Even after she was gone, most of us didn't know what to say.

Finally, someone broke the silence.

"What happened out here?" Ms. Matthews asked, surveying the scene while fiddling with the bandage on her finger.

Like Garbage Attracts Flies

The driver had broken three ribs, but I learned that from my mom, not from the news. Something else had managed to overshadow our superhero sighting.

About the same time that school was letting out and Ultraviolet was saving the two kids, alarms started blaring at the power plant outside of town. There had been a break-in.

Stories were all over the news, with each station trying to get some sort of advantage over the others. Every few minutes some reporter would pop up with words like EXCLUSIVE or BREAKING NEWS written in bright yellow letters across the screen. I spent hours watching reports on TV and reading them on the Internet, trying to piece together every detail I could. The next morning, the newspaper published a detailed account of the event.

Kanigher Falls Gazette

ARMORED ROBBERY AT POWER PLANT

Police Trying to Identify Possible Supervillain

Yesterday, at approximately three in the afternoon, a man in mechanical armor approached the entrance gate of the Palo Dini Nuclear Generating Station. As guards approached the man, he leapt over the gate and proceeded to run toward the plant's primary cooling tower. When the man failed to obey a guard's orders to stop, another guard opened fire with his pistol, but the bullets bounced off the man's armor plating.

Witnesses said the man laughed and raised his hand, pulling the gun from the guard's hands with what authorities suspect is a powerful electromagnet embedded in the palm of the armor. According to another guard, the suspect then crushed the gun "the way you or I might crumple a piece of paper."

Several more security guards arrived at the scene, carrying much larger automatic weapons. The suspect reportedly demanded access to the plant's uranium rods. The security guards opened fire, but a hail of bullets left little more than tiny dents in the suspect's armor. On security camera footage, the man can be seen touching his left gauntlet, accessing what police suspect is a control panel built into the armored suit.

"The mechanics of the suit allow him to move extremely quickly and make him very powerful," said Camille LoDuca, a spokesperson for Palo Dini.

Some witnesses inside the plant reported seeing a small cylinder emerge from the back of his right hand. One bystander described it as looking "like a lipstick tube," but authorities have since identified it as a hyperpowered laser.

Clark Trammell, a scientist with Collins Laboratories in Darwyn City, explained that although they are highly experimental, hyperpowered lasers are capable of slicing through nearly any material on Earth, including the several-foot-thick concrete and steel walls of the nuclear reactor.

At this time, officials are not revealing the exact number of uranium rods that were stolen. However, one anonymous source speculated that the suspect might have taken as many as a dozen before he escaped using rockets embedded in his boots and the back of his armor.

Officials from the power plant explained that the

uranium rods normally fueled the reactor but could also be used to make a nuclear bomb.

In that light, the dump truck story was barely an afterthought.

In fact, a lot of people blamed Ultraviolet for not being at the power plant to stop the break-in. I even heard one radio talk-show host say that not only was it her fault for not stopping the guy, but she was also to blame for his showing up at all.

"Superheroes attract supervillains like garbage attracts flies," he snarled over the radio.

○ ○ ○

At school on Monday, nearly a third of the desks were empty. Evidently, lots of parents decided to keep their kids home because of the threat of a nuclear bomb. For a moment, I wished I'd tried to talk my dad into letting me skip school, too, but I realized he'd never have gone for it. I could just imagine his response.

"If a nuclear bomb goes off in this town, you're just as dead at home as you are at school, so you might as well go learn something," he'd say.

No one at school was talking about Ultraviolet. In fact, Dave Bargman was the only kid to bring her up, and that was just to put her down.

"Uh-oh, looks like Ultraviolet let you down, huh?" he teased as we walked into history class.

"How?" I snapped. "When she saved two kids from becoming pavement pizzas?"

"No, when she let some maniac break into the power plant." Ms. Matthews, who'd been writing on the blackboard, turned her head to listen to us. "I guess I was right when I said she wasn't much of a superhero."

"How do you figure?" I challenged.

"Phantom Ranger would never have let some dork in a power suit steal stuff to make a nuclear bomb," Dave replied.

"Three months ago, Phantom Ranger had his power belt stolen by Coldsnap!" I fired back. I had nothing against Phantom Ranger, but even I could acknowledge that that had been a dumb move.

"He got it back!" Dave insisted.

"Yeah," I agreed. "But that was *after* Coldsnap leveled the Schigiel Building."

Ms. Matthews interrupted us. "Boys, you know how I feel about all this superhero nonsense in my room." She turned back to the board, then wheeled around again.

"Nate, weren't you saying in your speech that we don't need Ultraviolet?" she said. "The way I see it, this incident is just helping everyone else realize that, too."

"No, that wasn't the point at all," I insisted. "I meant that we can't rely on superheroes to do everything. If Ultraviolet had stopped the power plant heist, those two kids would be dead, and people would blame her for that instead. Sure, Phantom Ranger got his belt back and he rebuilt the building, but for a while, things were looking pretty bad. The people of Darwyn City didn't blame him, though. We should have the same faith and stand behind Ultraviolet the same way!"

Dave and Ms. Matthews seemed to be thinking over my point, but then the bell rang and the subject was dropped.

The only person who seemed the least bit sympathetic to Ultraviolet was Dr. Content. When he overheard two kids in the back of science class talking about her, he cut into their conversation.

"It's not her fault," he explained. "I used to work at that power plant, and I assure you, the blame lies squarely with the regulatory commission. I warned them more times than I can count—and being a nuclear engineer, I can count pretty high—that they needed to tighten up security or something like this would happen someday."

And with that, he fired up the computer slide show and started his lesson on food chains.

After class, Dr. Content asked me to stay behind. "How goes the project?" he asked, smiling broadly. "Any headway on cracking the case?"

"Oh." I looked at the floor. "Not really."

"I thought you had a pretty good lead," he said.

"Yeah, but it turned out to be a dead end."

Dr. Content looked disappointed, but then he brightened up almost immediately. "Welcome to the world of science, Mr. Banks," he said. "Every theory is based on a hypothesis that has to be proven. Sometimes, hypotheses are proven false. That doesn't necessarily mean you're wrong. You just have to find another approach."

"I'm pretty sure I was wrong," I pointed out.

"That just means you have to reexamine your evidence and see where else it might lead," Dr. Content insisted. "On top of that, you should have some new evidence now. What did you observe when you saw Ultraviolet in person?"

I tried to run through the scene in my head again, but nothing important came to mind. "I don't know," I said with a shrug. "She seems invulnerable; she's strong; she flies . . . all stuff I already knew. I got a better look at her costume, but I didn't see anything that would help me crack her secret identity. Why? Did *you* see something I should have noticed?"

"No, I missed the whole thing," he replied. "I had to leave school early to run an errand. I just don't want you to give up so easily, Nate. Now, don't be late to lunch."

○ ○ ○

After dinner, Mom asked how I was doing with my extra-credit science project. I described my conversation with Dr. Content.

"I understand he wants to make science more hands-on," I explained. "And I see how using the scientific method can help me organize my thoughts. But now it seems pretty silly to think I could actually figure out Ultraviolet's secret identity. Dr. Content wants me to continue with it, though."

"He just wants to make sure you stick it out," Dad said while he scraped our plates. "He doesn't really expect you to discover her identity. He just wants you to show evidence that you organized your facts." He tied up the garbage bag and handed it to me.

"In that case, I need better evidence," I argued. "Real scientists get a chance to observe their studies in person."

"Not paleontologists," my sister pointed out. "Dinosaurs have been dead for millions of years and paleontologists still manage to study them."

"Paleontologists," I grumbled as I walked through my

backyard with the garbage. "Does Ultraviolet look like a dinosaur to you?"

I ducked under the branches of the oak tree next to the fence, pushed open the gate, and stepped into the alley, tossing the bag into the large black can.

I started back toward the house, but something felt strange, like I wasn't alone. I looked down the alley, but I couldn't see anyone. I opened the lid to the trash can again to make sure no one was hiding inside. Nothing.

I shrugged and made my way back through the gate and into my yard. Still the weird feeling remained. I scanned my yard but saw nothing.

"Looking for me?" a woman called from above. I almost leapt out of my skin. I looked up into the oak tree and saw Ultraviolet sitting on a branch.

"I didn't mean to startle you, Nate," she apologized. "I just needed to ask you a few questions."

The Right Person for the Job

Ultraviolet drifted slowly down from her perch and landed beside me on the grass. "Close your mouth or a bug's going to fly in there," she said with a smile.

I realized that my face had gone completely slack. My jaw was hanging open, and my eyes wouldn't blink no matter how hard I tried to force them.

"I heard you're the one to talk to around here about superheroics," she began. "At least, that's what I figured from that picture behind the counter at the comic-book store."

"I—I won a contest," I stammered.

"I gathered." She smiled reassuringly. "You don't have to be nervous, Nate. I just wanted to pick your brain a little bit. There are a lot of people in this town saying I should quit."

"No," I corrected her, finally finding the ability to speak, "there are a lot of people being put on the news because they're saying you should quit. There's a difference."

"I suppose that's a good way to look at it," she mused. "It's just hard for me to tell if I'm any good at this."

Dumbfounded, I examined her from head to toe while replaying the scene of the dump truck rescue in my brain.

"Are you kidding me?" I asked. "You're great! You flew right in front of that truck without hesitating. You're brave and stro—"

"No," she interrupted. "I'm not brave, Nate. Brave is when you risk your life to do something that needs to be done. When I flew in front of that truck, I knew it wouldn't hurt me. I haven't been hurt by anything since my powers manifested themselves when I was eight years old."

"All right, so you're noble instead of brave," I said. "There's not much difference."

"I think there is," she continued. "I do what I do because it's the right thing to do. It's polite. I've always tried to help people out whenever I could, but I never wanted to put on a costume and fly around. But then, a few weeks ago, this guy came up to me and—"

She stopped herself. The look on her face told me she might have already said too much.

"Let me put it this way." She tried again. "If you had a dozen or so quarters and I gave you a dollar, you'd make change for me, right?"

"Yeah," I said with a shrug. "So?"

"Well, to me, flying into a burning building is the same thing," she said. "It's just something I do because I can, but that doesn't make me a hero. A fireman who runs into that same building knowing he could be burned alive or crushed by falling support beams is a hero."

"You're being too hard on yourself," I told her. "Nobody's questioning your bravery."

"No, I do that myself," she said. "Because I've never been hurt before, I have no idea how I'll react when I'm in a situation where I *can* be hurt. I'm still pretty new to this superhero thing, and there's no training manual to read or classes to take."

I don't know which was stranger: having Ultraviolet in my yard or learning that she was as confident about her superheroic powers as I was about my math skills.

"I just wanted to lend police a hand and keep people safe, but I don't think I'm cut out for—" She stopped herself again. "Somewhere in this city, there is a guy in a suit of armor who may or may not have a nuclear bomb. Even if he doesn't, at some point, he's going to rob a bank or raid the downtown jewelry district or attack the city council. And, according to the reports from the power plant, he just may be a match for me, power-wise."

"You're not the first superhero to face a nemesis of equal or greater power," I reassured her. "Just look at Captain Zombie. Who *isn't* more powerful than him? And all Zilch can do is change the way he looks. But they both still manage to save the day . . . well, most of the time, anyway."

Ultraviolet chuckled. "Good point." She got a thoughtful look on her face. "I guess I just haven't been nervous in a long time. I kind of forgot what it's like."

"You want to talk about nervous? I had to give a speech at school on Thursday and I hate giv — never mind." It dawned on me how stupid I probably sounded comparing a student council campaign speech to fighting a master criminal with a nuclear bomb.

"No, go on," she said. "What was the speech about?"

"I was running for student council vice president and I told everyone that superheroes aren't special because of their powers, but because of what they do. You know — they help people."

Ultraviolet smiled. "Sounds like a great speech," she said. "Wish I could have been there to hear it."

"So do I," I laughed, thinking about my mom's

experience with Phantom Ranger. "Maybe someone would have actually voted for me."

"Don't tell your teacher I said this, but student council elections are nothing but popularity contests," she said. "Just because you're not the most popular, that doesn't mean you're not the right person for the job."

"I could say the same thing to you," I said with a shrug.

"I suppose so," she agreed. "Now, I have to go find that uranium."

"Yeah!" I cheered. "Then the news stations will have to go back to reporting the good stuff you do."

"I was more concerned with saving the city from nuclear annihilation," she replied.

"Both are good," I agreed.

"Now get inside and do your homework," she said as she lifted off into the air.

I took a deep breath and then bolted for the house, my finger already poised to dial Teddy's phone number.

Introducing the Content X-1

Kanigher Falls Gazette

POLICE BLOTTER

A mugger holding a knife confronted a couple walking from the Kubert Cinemas movie theater on Baron Road to their car at approximately 9:50 p.m. Monday night. The victims reported that before they could reach for their wallets, Ultraviolet swept down from the sky, grabbed the mugger by his collar, and then flew back up over the rooftops without slowing. The suspect was found tied to the railing of the front steps of the nearest police station.

Two men were extracted from a tunnel beneath the Eighth National Bank at 10:41 p.m. Monday night. Further investigation indicates that the men began digging the tunnel earlier that afternoon, starting in the back room of a barbecue restaurant across the parking lot. Ultraviolet removed the men from the tunnel and turned them over to the authorities.

A man who fell asleep behind the wheel of his car while crossing the Schaffenberger Bridge suffered only minor scratches and bruises due to Ultraviolet's intervention. A witness saw the car strike the guardrail at approximately 11:20 p.m. Monday night, but reported that it was lifted out of harm's way just before it collided with an oncoming vehicle. The driver was treated at Kanigher Falls General Hospital and was later released.

•

Of course, all these stories were buried on the back page of the next morning's newspaper in the police blotter, right next to minutes from the city zoning commission meeting. The front-page story, which dominated the TV and radio news as well, was about how police were still baffled by the uranium theft. According to the paper, the FBI was refusing to comment, and Ultraviolet still hadn't nabbed the bad guy.

As Teddy, Fiona, and I approached the school crosswalk, we overheard a lot of people talking about it.

"My dad thinks the mayor is going to call Wildblaze to come in from Lenwein," someone said.

"I'm telling you, only Phantom Ranger can handle this," Dave Bargman insisted.

"They should get Zilch to help," offered a tiny boy who was listening in.

"Zilch?" Robby Baker groaned. "What's he going to do? Make himself look like some uranium and hope he gets stolen?"

"Ultraviolet is going to catch this guy!" Fiona shouted over them. "Last night she told Na—"

I grabbed her by the shoulder to stop her.

"What?" she asked.

I pulled her and Teddy aside. "I'm already the crazy kid who's obsessed with superheroes," I whispered. "I don't need to be the crazy kid who thinks he sees superheroes in his backyard, too."

"Aw, man, you can't be serious!" Teddy whined. "We have to tell people. This is huge!"

"Just keep it quiet for a little while," I said. "Please?"

My friends reluctantly agreed, but I hadn't yet thought about what I was going to say to the other person who'd be curious about my conversation: Dr. Content.

And I wouldn't have much time to figure it out, either.

"Mr. Banks!" Dr. Content greeted me in the parking lot. "How goes the project?"

"I'll catch up with you guys later," I said to my friends. I walked over to Dr. Content. He seemed to be struggling to carry what looked like a very heavy briefcase.

"It's going . . . um . . . ," I stammered. "I have some new data to include in my . . . uh . . . observations."

"That's interesting," he said, nodding enthusiastically. "Walk with me and tell me more."

I followed him to his classroom, where he hefted his briefcase onto the desk and sat down, looking eager to hear what I had to say.

"Ultraviolet contacted me last night," I blurted out, trying to sound professional and scientific, but failing miserably. "She came to my house."

Dr. Content's jaw dropped. "You say she sought you out?"

"Yes. I was just taking out the trash and there she was, waiting for me."

He leaned forward. "Remarkable! Go on."

"She wanted to ask me some questions . . . about being a superhero."

"Really?" he gasped. "And what did you tell her?"

"Just that she's doing a good job," I continued. "She was kind of nervous about that guy in the power armor—"

"Fascinating," he said. "So she thinks he's . . . what?"

"I don't know. I guess just that he's pretty powerful and she doesn't know if she can take him on."

"So Ultraviolet isn't as confident as one might think." He shook his head, stood up, and opened his briefcase. "This just blows me away, Nate. Great job!"

He reached into his briefcase and pulled out a metallic cylinder that looked like a soda can. From the way he lifted it, though, I could tell that it was much heavier than a Diet Coke. He set it on the desk with a dull thud, smiling the entire time.

"And what observations did you make regarding her identity?" he asked.

"I hadn't really thought about it," I replied. "She's a bit shorter than I might have thought at first, only about five six, maybe five seven—"

"Did she indicate how she found you?" he prodded.

"No, but she knew where I lived," I said. "I guess she just followed me."

"Or she's been watching you," Dr. Content suggested.

"I was wondering that myself," I admitted. "But I don't know if she's been watching me, or if she has some kind of supersense that allows her to watch and listen to everybody at once."

Dr. Content picked up the soda can–like object and motioned for me to follow him into the class laboratory.

"If she's been watching you and following you home, you probably wouldn't have too much trouble finding her or getting in touch with her if you really wanted to." He started adjusting some knobs on a large piece of machinery in a corner of the lab. "Do you think you could get her to meet you again?"

While he fiddled with the machine, I picked up the can. I was surprised by how heavy it was.

"I don't know," I answered. "I guess I could try. What's in this can?"

Dr. Content ignored my question. "If you could get her to meet with you again, you could prepare a complete list of questions and really learn more about her," he said. He took the can from me and opened a small hatch on the side of the machine that was just the right size for it. He held the dull metal cylinder up in the air and smiled at me.

"For the record, Nate, this is uranium," he said. Then he dropped it into the hatch, sealed it, and flipped a switch. A disturbing hum filled the room.

"To be more accurate, that was a uranium containment unit," Dr. Content went on. "I don't want you to worry about radiation. We're perfectly safe now that it's sealed in here." He patted the hatch reassuringly.

The lights on the machine started to brighten the room, giving me my first glimpse of what Dr. Content's machine really was.

"That's power armor!" I gasped.

"Hardly." He sighed. "Calling this power armor is like calling a Mercedes-Benz a 'car.' This is my own creation, and it's more powerful than any single machine on Earth. The key is the generator."

He pointed to the back of the armor, which was where he'd deposited the can a moment earlier.

"When I originally designed this armor, it quickly became apparent that it would need a lot of power," he explained. "The propulsion engines, electromagnets, and pulse beams that are required to move the arms and legs around would drain a car battery in less than a minute. I needed a generator that could produce the necessary power."

He unbuttoned his shirt and slipped into the armor, attaching sensors to his chest and arms.

"While I was working at the power plant, I designed a nuclear generator small enough to fit in a suitcase," he continued. "I wanted to build a prototype, but my colleagues told me it was too dangerous, and that something so small would be too unstable.

"I started to build the generator anyway—the Content X-1—until I was discovered. Despite my protests, the regulatory commission fired me. Fortunately, I was able to smuggle out the parts I needed to complete the project."

"Except for the uranium," I realized aloud.

"Exactly," he noted as the armor clicked into place. "I managed to get some low-grade radioactive materials, but just enough to power the suit so that I could get into the plant, get the uranium, and get out. I was lucky. Two more minutes and I would have been stuck there like a driver whose car ran out of gas on an empty stretch of highway."

"But why?" I asked.

"Why what?"

"Why build this suit?"

"I figured that much was obvious, especially to someone like you." He smiled and paused for dramatic effect. "I wanted to be a superhero."

I stared at him, unsure how to react.

"Nate, you and I are alike. We both want to be superheroes, but neither one of us has superpowers. I spent my life learning the sciences I needed to know to make this armor work. I spent more than a decade building it, piece by piece. This gauntlet alone took me two years to complete." He raised his metallic glove into the air.

"I had to program a navigational computer, learn how to fly, and create a whole new form of propulsion. Then I made a generator that could power a city and fit in a backpack."

Dr. Content opened a panel on his left gauntlet, revealing a keypad. After he touched a few of the buttons, the suit lurched forward and he started walking toward me. He swept his metallic arm around the room dramatically.

"I created all this, and yet here I am teaching sixth graders the difference between igneous and sedimentary rocks," he said. "Still, I told myself it would all be worth it when I could soar over the skies of Kanigher Falls, saving lives, stopping crimes, and being cheered by the masses."

His smile twisted into a bitter sneer. "Unfortunately, a little someone called Ultraviolet came along and ruined that for me."

"How did she ruin it?" I asked.

"Nate, you know as well as I do there can't be more than one iconic superhero in a city. I worked hard to be that hero for this city, but before I could finish my project, she showed up with power that you or I would give anything to have! Now you're telling me she isn't even sure she knows how to be a superhero! It's too late for me, though. If I went out there now, people would just think of me as a copycat—or, worse, her sidekick."

I began inching toward the door, but I didn't see how it would help. I had no idea how to escape from a delusional madman with lasers, jet engines, and a nuclear generator strapped to his back.

"No, Ultraviolet made her choice," he continued. "And when she decided to be this town's hero, it became obvious what my role was going to be. I would have to be a supervillain. Her nemesis."

He plugged a wire from his suit into a headpiece and smiled at the completed transformation.

"My parents named me Malcolm Content!" he boomed. "Maybe they knew this was my fate all along. From now on, you can call me Dr. Malcontent."

"Malcontent?"

"*Doctor* Malcontent, please," he corrected me. "I spent six years earning that degree."

"Sorry, *Doctor* Malcontent," I said. "Anyway, I really need to get to class or I'm going to be marked late and my parents will ground me—"

"Oh, I'll give you a late slip," he assured me. "I just need your help with my project first."

"Um . . . all right," I agreed warily. I didn't know what would happen if I said no. "What do you need me to do?"

"You're going to be bait," he answered plainly. Before I could even blink, he leapt across the classroom and grabbed me by the throat with his massive metallic hand. "Now, let's go see how closely Ultraviolet is watching you."

Get a Grip, Doc

I struggled for only about three seconds before I realized it was a pointless exercise. Dr. Malcontent gripped my neck with fingers powerful enough to flip a Cadillac the way anyone else would a quarter. He tucked my chest under the sleek, metal arm like I was a football and he was a running back on his way to the end zone. This left my legs free to kick, but it quickly became apparent that wasn't going to do me any good.

I was going nowhere.

Unfortunately, Dr. Malcontent didn't seem to know where he was going, either. He lurched clumsily down the hallway, pivoting every few steps in case Ultraviolet was sneaking up on him.

"What can you do to draw her out?" he asked me.

"I don't know," I grunted through my compressed throat.

He continued his cautious progress down the hall. "If she's keeping an eye on you, she'll probably be waiting outside the school," he finally decided. "That's where I'll spring my tra—"

"Nathan Banks, you are late," Ms. Matthews interrupted from behind us. Dr. Malcontent spun to face her. He raised his free hand and pointed the pulse beam directly at her chest. Her eyes were still on me, and she appeared to be completely oblivious to the lumbering cybernetic beast who held me in his grasp. "The bells are not a *suggestion*, young man." She pointed to the clock in the hallway.

"Stay out of my way," Dr. Malcontent sneered.

Slowly, her eyes turned to Dr. Malcontent, as if she'd just noticed he was there. While most people would have run screaming at the sight of a man in mechanized armor, Ms. Matthews just shook her head in disappointment.

"Malcolm, you know better than to keep students out of class."

"Get back in your room, Sophie!" he threatened.

She clucked her tongue and stepped toward us, reaching out as if to drag me away from him.

"I'm not kidding!" Dr. Malcontent shouted. "Stay back!" He swung his free arm at her, knocking her into a bank of lockers. I gasped when I saw the huge dent in the locker doors, and I almost couldn't believe it when she got up and stumbled toward us again.

"Malcolm . . ." She shook her head and reached toward me again.

"I didn't want to have to do this!" Dr. Malcontent yelled. The next thing I knew, I heard the blast of his pulse beam. The intensity of the burst made my eyes go all spotty, and it was hard to see for a few seconds.

Ms. Matthews was tossed backward again, this time through a cinder-block wall. There was no trace of her. It was as if she'd been vaporized into nothingness.

I swallowed hard, straining against the mechanical hand at my throat. Part of me felt bad that Ms. Matthews had given her life trying to help me. But a bigger part worried what Dr. Malcontent would do next.

The fire sprinklers burst into action, which helped to settle some of the dust. The blast had made a hole in the wall of the classroom in front of me, and the students inside were scrambling to get away. I watched them clamber over piles of broken concrete as they escaped. The sprinklers must have triggered the fire alarm, warning any classes that hadn't heard or felt the explosion to evacuate.

"Let's get out of here!" Dr. Malcontent shouted over

the alarm as he ran down the hallway with loud, clumsy stomps.

As we neared the principal's office, there was a voice behind us.

"Don't you know there's no running in the halls?"

Dr. Malcontent spun around so that we were facing Ultraviolet as she stepped through the hole in the wall. She was coated in a thin layer of plaster.

"Finally!" he boomed. "I've been looking forward to meeting you, Ultraviolet."

"I can't say the same," she replied.

"That's right," he said with a smile. "My buddy Nate here told me you're afraid of me."

"I didn't tell him that, Ultr—" I tried to yell, but Dr. Malcontent's hand squeezed my throat shut.

"Don't worry about it, Nate," she reassured me. Then she turned to face Dr. Malcontent. "The only thing I'm afraid of is that you'll do something stupid and someone will get hurt."

"If you wanted to make sure no one got hurt, you're a little late," he chuckled. "Feel free to pick through that rubble back there and see if you can find a mousy little history teacher who didn't know how to mind her own business. She might not be dead yet."

As Ultraviolet began walking toward us, Dr.

Malcontent picked me up, raising me closer to his face. "Be careful, superhero. I've got your little advisor here. I wouldn't want anything to happen to him because you got careless."

"What do you want, Content?" she asked icily.

"Oh, Malcolm Content doesn't exist anymore. You're dealing with Dr. Malcontent now."

"Put the boy down, Malcont—"

"Doctor!" he shouted. "It's *Doctor* Malcontent!"

Ultraviolet sighed deeply. "I really don't have the patience for all this superhero-supervillain banter. Put the kid down, shut off that ridiculous suit, and turn over the nuke. Now."

"There is no nuke!" I tried to shout. "The uranium's for his suit!" Unfortunately, Dr. Malcontent's vise grip on my throat turned my warning into an incoherent whisper.

"I don't need to make threats with bombs!" he shouted back. "I made better use of that uranium than any of those narrow-minded scientists at the power plant ever could have imagined! I harnessed its power and made it my own, and now *I'm* the most powerful one in this town."

"And yet you're still hiding behind a sixth grader," Ultraviolet countered.

The next thing I knew, I was lying in a crumpled heap

beside a trophy case near Principal Gwynn's office. Dr. Malcontent flipped open the control panel on his left gauntlet and pressed a sequence of buttons.

Faster than my brain could register, Ultraviolet streaked down the hallway toward him. But some kind of radar-activated countermeasure in Dr. Malcontent's armor registered her advance, calculated her angle and rate of approach, and activated a defensive mode. His arm cocked back and punched her just as she struck him.

The sound was deafening. The glass in the trophy case shattered, raining tiny shards on my head and on the floor around me. When I opened my eyes, I could see both of them getting up off the ground. They seemed amazed at the impact they had endured.

Dr. Malcontent rushed Ultraviolet this time, pummeling her with a blur of punches. I could feel the shock waves in my chest even from twenty feet away. She fended off a few of his blows, but it was clear—just as she'd said in my backyard the night before—that she wasn't accustomed to facing an opponent who could match her speed and strength.

She didn't look frightened, but I worried she might be too overwhelmed for the fear to even register. She was trying her best to shield herself with both arms as she carefully got her footing beneath her.

For a split second, she looked directly at me and smiled. Then she hurled herself at Dr. Malcontent's chest, wrapped her arms around him, and flew down the hall and out the double-door entrance. It happened so fast all I saw was a purple and white blur.

I staggered to my feet and surveyed the scene. Tiles hung from the ceiling like loose teeth, just waiting to fall. Rows of lockers had crumpled like candy wrappers. Most of the lights had shattered, leaving the hall dark, lit only by the sunlight that streamed in through holes in the walls.

Shaking the shards of glass from my hair, I ran after Dr. Malcontent and Ultraviolet. One of the double doors still hung by a single hinge. The other lay on the sidewalk about ten yards away. I didn't see either of them at first, but I noticed all the students standing together in clusters—as we were taught to do during fire drills—craning their necks to look at the sky.

I looked up and saw Ultraviolet unleashing her own beating on Dr. Malcontent. In the air, he was at her mercy. The tables had completely reversed from the close quarters of the hallway.

That is, until he managed to level a single punch that seemed to carry the force of a wrecking ball. Ultraviolet reeled and he separated from her, which sent him into free fall. Calmly, he flipped open the panel on his left forearm and pressed a button, bringing small jets in his boots roaring to life.

In an instant, they were evenly matched again.

"Nate!" Teddy shouted. "Over here!"

He and Fiona were standing with our classmates. I ran over to join them.

"Are you okay?" Fiona asked.

"I guess so," I told her. Honestly, I hadn't even stopped to think about it. Considering I could still walk and hadn't been crushed beneath a crumbling wall or sliced to ribbons by shattered glass, I assumed I was fine.

"We kind of figured you were dead," Teddy admitted. Then he threw his arms around me in an awkward bear hug. I did my best to pat him on the back, but couldn't quite manage, since he'd pinned my arms to my sides.

Fiona rolled her eyes. "Would you knock it off, Teddy?" she said. "You're making a scene."

"What happened in there?" Teddy asked as he released me from his grip.

"Dr. Content built a suit of nuclear-powered armor that makes him as fast and as strong as Ultraviolet. They pretty much trashed the inside of the school."

"Does that mean we'll get a day off?" Teddy asked.

Before I could answer, the police showed up, with the

news vans not far behind. Reporters scrambled to get their cameras set up while police did their best to move the students off campus to a safe area.

Ultraviolet and Dr. Malcontent maneuvered around each other like planes in a dogfight. As I watched their deadly dance in the clouds, two things occurred to me. First, Dr. Malcontent's pulse beams gave him a distinct advantage. He could continue to blast at Ultraviolet with disintegrating rays. She'd avoided the blasts so far, but I didn't know how much longer her luck would last.

Second, Dr. Malcontent's suit was powered by a nuclear reactor, but he was a human and would have to rest eventually. Assuming that Ultraviolet had greater superendurance and could maintain her focus longer, I thought she might be able to defeat him just by outlasting him.

They continued to grapple, each trying to steer the other in the opposite direction. They were deadlocked, and Dr. Malcontent attempted to take the battle back to solid ground. While still entwined with Ultraviolet, he hit another button on his control panel, reversing the armor's thrusters and sending them both rocketing toward the school again.

They crashed through the roof with such force that they broke through the building's foundation and several hundred feet of bedrock. Dozens of kids lost their balance as the ground shook. Car alarms throughout the neighborhood went off at once.

"Kids, I need you to follow me across the street," a policeman urged us. He pointed to an area where barricades were being erected around a row of cop cars and SWAT vans. We started to follow him across the baseball field when I heard a rumbling behind us. I turned around to look and nearly tripped over Meathead McCaskill.

He sat on the grass, rocking and whimpering, his knees tucked to his chest.

Dr. Malcontent rose slowly from the hole in the heart of the school and hovered toward us.

"Here he comes!" the policeman shouted as he hustled us along. "Move quickly, kids!"

I grabbed Meathead under the arms to lift him to his feet. "Come on, Angus," I grunted as I dragged him toward the barricades.

"Mommy?" he whimpered.

A police officer ran over to help me carry Meathead as Dr. Malcontent flew our way, but it was soon evident that we weren't Dr. Malcontent's targets.

Instead, he was headed for the news reporters and their cameras. "Take a good look, Kanigher Falls!" he shouted dramatically. "The champion you've embraced has met her match!"

He flipped open his control panel again and lowered himself to the ground. My classmates kept running for safety, but suddenly, I froze in my tracks. All at once, it occurred to me: I knew how to defeat Dr. Malcontent. I just had to get that information to Ultraviolet.

"I am Dr. Malcontent," he said to the cameras. "Learn my name well, for you shall scream it in your nightmares."

I sprinted back toward the school, hoping to see Ultraviolet emerge from the piles of broken concrete and wiring. The policeman carrying Meathead shouted something and his partner came chasing after me. I knew I couldn't outrun him, but I needed to get my message to Ultraviolet.

A smiling Dr. Malcontent saw us running and decided to demonstrate the power of his armor for the press. He engaged the electromagnets in his fists and lifted one of the police cars from the faculty parking lot, then tossed it toward the officer. It landed just a few feet in front of him. The officer nearly tripped over himself as he came to a stop.

Ahead of me, Ultraviolet burst from the wreckage of the school.

"Ultraviolet!" I screamed. "I know how to stop him!" But my words were drowned out by the sirens, falling debris, and the general chaos of hundreds of panicked people trying not to get killed.

She rose about thirty feet in the air before coming to a stop and looking down at me. "Nate?" she asked as she lowered herself toward the ground. "Why are you still here?"

"I figured out what you need to do—" I started to explain.

She sighed and pushed her goggles up the bridge of her nose in a move I'd seen way too many times not to recognize. I'd been right all along.

"Nate, do you realize how irresponsible it is for you to be—"

"Ms. Matthews?" I gasped.

Before she could respond, I felt myself being grabbed from behind. At first I thought it was the policeman, but then I quickly registered the dull hum of Dr. Malcontent's generator and the cold grip of his gauntlet around my throat.

The gauntlet! In my shock, I had forgotten to tell Ms. Matthews how to defeat Dr. Malcontent.

Someone's Got to Take the Fall

"This is getting tiresome," Dr. Malcontent grumbled. "I'm trying to hold a press conference over there and the two of you are causing a distraction." He smiled up at Ultraviolet. "Nate is in my science class, and he can tell you that I don't like people talking when I'm trying to talk."

"Put him down, Mal—*Doctor* Malcontent," she growled. "This doesn't involve him."

"That's where you're wrong. I trusted this kid. I thought he'd be my ticket to beating you. The thing is, he still can be—since I know as long as I have a grip on him you'll never attack me."

Ultraviolet said nothing.

"I, on the other hand, have no such qualms about attacking you." He laughed as he fired a pulse blast from his palm, hitting her square in the chest. The impact threw her into one of the few remaining school walls.

Groggily, she stumbled back to her feet. Her goggles had been knocked askew, and I saw her readjust them before she faced Dr. Malcontent again.

Frustrated, he dropped me into a pile of rubble to free up both hands. Then he fired the left and right pulse beams together. The force knocked Ultraviolet back to the ground. She lay still for a few seconds while Dr. Malcontent's weapons recharged, but then she struggled to one knee and ultimately rose to her feet again.

"We could keep doing this all day," he whined. Then he reached down and grabbed me by the shirt. I clawed at the chunks of rubble, trying to get away, but there was nothing I could do. Soon he had locked his left arm around my neck again.

He placed his right palm against my cheek.

"These blasts may not be enough to kill you, but I don't think this kid is going to be able to say the same!" he shouted to Ultraviolet.

I could feel the pulse beam warming up against my face. Desperately, I pulled at the metal fingers squeezing my throat. The arm wouldn't budge. All I could manage to do was open the small cover of the control panel.

"There's no point in fighting, Nate," Dr. Malcontent assured me. "That arm's not moving an inch."

"That's what I'm counting on," I muttered. My campaign speech echoed in my brain: *Superheroes do those great things for us, but we can't just sit around waiting for them to fix all our problems. Sometimes we have to be superheroes ourselves.*

With the control panel open, I randomly pressed any buttons I could get my fingers on. Then I smashed the panel repeatedly with a chunk of brick I'd grabbed when Dr. Malcontent had lifted me from the pile of rubble.

Sparks flew from the gauntlet and Dr. Malcontent dropped me immediately so that he could assess the damage. Desperately, he tried to press the shattered buttons and stop his out-of-control armor. The gauges and digital readouts on his helmet began flashing red, making his head look like a police car light.

Suddenly, he lurched off the ground and flew into a tree. The suit spun him in circles. He crashed into a basketball hoop, rocketed about two hundred feet into the air, and dove back to the ground.

He thrashed about on the grass, fighting against his own armor. When he finally got to his feet, he angrily pointed at me and shouted—

Well, he never got the chance to shout. Instead, the second he opened his mouth, Ultraviolet's fist hit his chest hard enough to register on the Richter scale.

Dr. Malcontent's armor cracked open. My science teacher's eyes rolled into the back of his head. As the alarms on the suit continued to blare and flash, he toppled to the ground, landing face-first in the grass.

The police started toward us, their guns drawn.

"Is he dead?" I asked Ultraviolet.

"No," Ultraviolet assured me. "I made sure I only hit the armor."

I looked at her closely. When she had the goggles on, I could barely see the woman who'd taught me about the Continental Congress. "I can't believe I fell for that paper-cut trick," I told her.

She smiled. "I got the idea from one of your comic—"

Suddenly, the armor moved. Ultraviolet swept me to the side, putting herself between me and the armor.

There was a muffled voice coming from inside the suit, but none of us could understand it. The armor whined as Dr. Malcontent pulled off the broken helmet.

"Think you stopped me?" he hissed. "You may have beaten me for now, but I'm still going to win."

The alarms on his suit grew louder and higher-pitched, sounding more and more urgent. "What's wrong with it?" I asked.

"The containment unit," Dr. Malcontent whispered. He rose to his knees and jerked his thumb toward his back. "It's cracked." He looked me in the eye. He seemed more disappointed than threatening. "I guess those other engineers at the plant were right."

"What is he talking about?" Ultraviolet asked me.

"The scientists he used to work with all told him this thing was too dangerous, because it would be unstable," I explained. I stepped forward and pointed to the cracks in the armor.

"You've got about two minutes until it goes critical," he warned us. His hand lashed out, grabbed my shirt, and pulled me close until his face was inches from my own. "And in two and a half, this city will be a crater."

The next thing I knew, everything vanished in a rushing howl. But what I thought was an atomic explosion proved to be something even scarier. I quickly deduced that I couldn't see or hear because I was being blasted by tornado-force winds. My ears popped and popped again, more times than I could count.

Dizzy and sickened, I pried my eyes open. The first thing I could make out in a blurry haze was the menacing fist of Dr. Malcontent tightly gripping my shirt and pulling me upward. Beyond that, I struggled to focus, but I could see Ultraviolet's gloved hands hooked under his arms and lifting him up.

I turned my face away from the gusts of wind and

looked at my feet. All I saw beneath them were clouds. Instinctively, I grasped Dr. Malcontent's metallic arm, no longer finding it nearly as threatening as the potential of my shirt tearing. It was only then that I started to understand what was happening.

So this was what it felt like to fly at supersonic speeds.

Even over the roar of our ascent through the stratosphere, I could hear Dr. Malcontent laughing maniacally. "A high-atmosphere nuclear detonation will be worse than a ground detonation. The wind will carry the radiation for miles. You'll kill ten times as many people this way."

Ultraviolet refused to respond, concentrating all her energy on flying faster until she reached the upper atmosphere. The winds against my eardrums quieted, not because she was slowing down, but because the air was thinning. Icy cold penetrated my body, but no matter how hard I shivered, I didn't dare lose my grip on the metal armor that was growing ice crystals. My vision grew darker, both because the lack of oxygen was robbing me of consciousness and because the darkness of space was coming into sight.

"You're going to hurl me into space?" Dr. Malcontent

snorted. "Some superhero you are. That's cold-blooded murder."

At once, she came to a stop, just as the air had thinned almost to the vacuum of space. She lifted Dr. Malcontent, who'd been hanging limply in her arms, so she could look him in the eyes, and she shook her head.

"No, I'm not going to throw you into space," she admitted.

I heard a shattering, twisting noise that sounded like a Dumpster being dropped inside my head. In one motion, Ultraviolet dug her fingers into the crack in his chest plate and peeled it open like it was a can of ravioli. Then she grabbed Dr. Malcontent's shoulder, yanked him out, and dropped him, letting him plummet back toward the Earth. His screams echoed in my ears as he fell.

Ultraviolet turned to me. With her free hand, she twisted apart the metal fist that held my shirt.

"Sorry, Nate," she said reluctantly. "This is the only way." Then she pushed my hands off the arm that I still gripped as my only lifeline. As I fell, I watched her fly up through the atmosphere into the nothingness of space, carrying the armor with her.

The familiar roar of the rushing wind filled my ears again, as did the rapid-fire sensation of swelling and popping that felt like someone playing with a sheet of bubble wrap inside my brain.

It was impossible to tell which way was up. I tried to spread myself out flat, thinking that this might slow me down, but it only made my arms and legs thrash about painfully, as though they were trying to break away from my torso and beat me to death. I pulled them in, which turned my body into something like a human bullet barreling toward the ground.

Frozen tears streaked my face as I struggled to see any details other than the clouds around me. Finally, I was able to lock on to one thing. Ahead of me, only a few hundred feet below, was a small balding man wearing nothing but boxer shorts. As we streaked downward, he would disappear behind clouds, only to reappear as I burst through them myself.

Finally, we broke through the last of the cloud cover. Beneath us, I could see Ditko Middle School, much of the wreckage from the fight still obscured by dust and smoke. The football field rocketed toward me, and a part of me morbidly wondered if I might die on the same spot where the three football players had nearly taken me out almost two weeks before.

Police and rescue workers on the field scrambled to get away from us, seemingly aware that there was nothing they could do but clean up the mess after we hit. I closed my eyes, certain I didn't want to see what would happen next, and prepared for the big splat.

Then something grabbed my ankle.

"I didn't want to hurt anyone," Dr. Malcontent shrieked. I opened my eyes to find myself face-to-face with him. "I just wanted to be a superhero! I just wanted . ."

He paused, as if realizing that he probably should have been dead by that point.

I looked around to see upside-down police approaching us. My hair brushed lightly against the grass of the forty-yard line. And to my left was a purple boot.

Ultraviolet floated inches off the ground, holding us both by the ankles as if she was a fisherman and we were prize trout.

Knowing we couldn't survive the vacuum of space, she'd had no choice but to let us go. I guessed she'd heaved the crippled armor into space and then headed back into the atmosphere after us. She gently lowered us to the grass. One of the police officers swooped in immediately to handcuff my science teacher and read him his rights.

"Malcolm Content, you have the right to remain silent. . . ."

Can You Keep a Secret?

Footage of the fight was all over the news for the next few days. There were images of exploding walls, of the flying police car, and of Ultraviolet holding me and a man in his underwear by the ankles. And then there was one video clip that showed Dr. Malcontent unleashing a blast from the palm of his hand, sending Ultraviolet into a wall. As she stood up, the cameraman zoomed in. A news editor had taken the shot, slowed it down, and digitally enhanced it so viewers could see Ultraviolet's face more closely as she adjusted her crooked goggles.

The picture was blurry, but it looked a lot like Ms. Matthews.

"While we cannot be certain, in this shot Ultraviolet looks very similar to Ms. Sophie Matthews, a history teacher at Ditko Middle School," a news anchor reported.

"Ms. Matthews's whereabouts could not be accounted for during the fight."

They froze the shot of Ultraviolet and put Ms. Matthews's school photo beside it.

"Some students and teachers claimed Ms. Matthews had been killed by the supervillain Dr. Malcontent prior to his battle with Ultraviolet," the anchor continued. "However, Ms. Matthews was later discovered across the street with evacuated students. She told police she had been there all along. Meanwhile, Malcolm Content, another teacher at Ditko Middle School, pleaded guilty to numerous charges stemming from his power-armor-driven rampage as Dr. Malcontent. He is being held and is awaiting sentencing."

Teddy got his wish. With the school in ruins, we did get a few days off before the superintendent decided to shuttle us to Eisner Middle School, a few miles away. We'd be finishing out the semester there while Ditko was rebuilt.

The downside to having unscheduled vacation time was that I couldn't talk to Ms. Matthews. All around town, people were accusing her of endangering her students, and demanding that she resign.

"This woman is the worst kind of irresponsible," the radio host blathered. "She uses the guise of helping our children only to put them at risk. This time, *only* a school fell victim to her superheroine game. Next time, who's to say there won't be bloodshed? Having her on the staff at this or any other school is like painting a big bull's-eye on the roof with a sign that says, 'Devest-8, strike here!' It's idiotic. She must be fired immediately!"

I switched off the radio and went out to the backyard, hoping I might randomly catch a glimpse of her. I'd been hanging out in my backyard for three days, watching the skies, but I hadn't had any luck. It had been nearly seventy-two hours since the fight, and I hadn't been able to speak with Ultraviolet at all. The next day, I would be back at school and I didn't know if she'd even be there.

I pushed aside some of the creeper vines, grabbed the trellis, and climbed to the roof of our house. I waved my arms and even tried doing jumping jacks before I realized that the thudding of my feet on the shingles would undoubtedly have my dad outside and yelling at me in no time.

"I take it you were trying to get my attention?" a voice behind me asked.

I turned to see Ultraviolet landing on the roof beside me. She sat down and took a deep breath, but said nothing.

I had so many things I wanted to say to her, but now

that she was next to me, I couldn't think of a single word. So we sat in silence.

"It was pretty smart of you to destroy his control panel," she finally said.

"Thanks," I replied. "I was trying to tell you about it, but he had me by the throat and . . . um . . . Is the school board going to let you keep teaching?"

"I don't know," she said with a sigh. "I haven't been answering my phone lately. Most of the calls are people either asking for autographs or wanting me to come to their kids' birthday parties or telling me what a horrible monster I am. A lot of people want me to quit teaching and leave town."

"That's going a little far," I said. "Even if you stop teaching, you'll still be Ultraviolet."

"Yeah, that's what I keep telling myself," she replied. She reached up and slid her goggles onto her forehead. "Remember what I said that one night, about how being a hero is just what I do because I can? Until the other day, I would have told you being a superhero is easy. And, with the exception of the occasional nuclear-powered science teacher, I guess it still is."

I laughed.

"But teaching isn't easy, Nate," she continued. "Teaching is something I do because I *want* to do it. I love teaching.

It's hard work and I go home some nights not knowing what to do, but when I figure it out, it's more rewarding than nabbing a thousand jewel thieves."

"There has to be something you can do," I offered weakly.

"The truth is, they're probably right," she continued. "Dr. Malcontent is just one bad guy out of thousands. If they know I'm a teacher, they're going to see you and all the other students as a bunch of potential hostages."

I touched my neck, which was still sore from Dr. Malcontent's powerful grip. I didn't know what to say.

"Wow!" a voice shouted from below. We both looked down to see my sister staring up at us. "When Nate said he thought you were Ultraviolet, I told him he was a moron." She turned to me and shrugged. "You're still a moron, but I can at least give credit where it's due."

"Denise, get out of here!" I yelled. "We're trying to have a serious conversation."

"Yeah, I know," she replied. "I've been down here on the porch listening for the last five minutes. You haven't offered any helpful info."

"Shut up, Denise!" I yelled back.

"This isn't one of your stupid comic books, Nate," she said. "Why don't you leave Ultraviolet alone so she can find someone who can really help her out?"

"You don't have any idea what you're talking abou—" I began.

As soon as Denise said the words "comic books," I had a brainstorm. I had just finished reading the latest issue of *Whirlwolf*, and Teddy's Internet rumor had been correct. The story *was* about Mr. Enigma threatening to reveal Whirlwolf's secret identity to the local newspaper. The issue ended with a cliff-hanger, but I already had a suspicion as to how the story would conclude in the next issue. Just like that, the solution to Ultraviolet's problem came to me.

"I know how we can save your job tomorrow," I told Ultraviolet excitedly. "How quickly can you get to Claremont and back?"

○ ○ ○

When we got to Eisner Middle School the next day, news vans filled the parking lot. Some parents were also outside, holding signs that said things like "Teach a lesson to our kids, not to criminals," and "We want teachers who are super, not superteachers."

The classrooms were only half full, even though we were sharing them with the students from Eisner. Many parents had kept their kids at home, refusing to let them attend until Ms. Matthews resigned or was fired.

Ms. Matthews had been in her classroom since five-thirty that morning just to avoid the media and the parents. I checked in with her when I arrived at school, to review our plan, but for the most part, I tried to treat it as just another day. I had to admit, though, that science class was a bit awkward and not as much fun with our substitute teacher, Mrs. Sutcliffe.

When I got to history, Ms. Matthews had an announcement to make.

"I didn't want to talk about this, but I know you've all heard some rumors about me and my—well, my being a superhero," she began. "There are a lot of parents and administrators asking me to leave my job because they worry I'm putting all of you in danger. I hope you all understand I would never do anything to endanger your—"

Suddenly, there was a knock at the door. We all looked up to see Ultraviolet peek into the room.

"I'm sorry to interrupt, Ms. Matthews," she said. "I understand how important your class time is, but do you think you could excuse Nate Banks for a moment?"

"It's Ultraviolet!" Teddy shouted as if he was reading from an index card. "Wow! And right here in Ms. Matthews's class!"

Fiona shook her head at Teddy's terrible acting.

"But I thought the news said Ms. Matthews *was*

Ultraviolet," Fiona said loudly. "I guess they were wrong."

Ms. Matthews waved her hand toward me, then followed me to the door, making sure the press gathered in the hallway outside saw her hand me over to Ultraviolet. Camera flashes went off like strobe lights as the two women stood side by side.

"Please don't keep him too long," Ms. Matthews said to Ultraviolet. "He has a quiz on the 1929 stock market crash in five minutes." Inside the room, the class groaned.

The reporters in the hallway seemed unsure of what they were seeing. Ultraviolet took advantage of their silence to introduce me. "This is Nate Banks, the young man who helped defeat Dr. Malcontent. He's one of Ms. Sophie Matthews's students, and I want him to get some of the credit for helping save the day."

"Is there anything you'd like to say, Nick?" one of the reporters asked.

"Uh, well, it's Nate," I began. "I just want to thank Ultraviolet, not only for saving the day, but also for inspiring all of us to be better people. And she's not the only one who does that. Ms. Matthews works very hard for her students, but she may have to quit because of some unproven rumors. I wish everyone would just leave Ms. Matthews alone and let her do her job."

Ms. Matthews smiled politely and turned to Ultraviolet. "Can I have him back now?" she asked.

"I think we're done here," Ultraviolet said to the reporters. "But I have to talk to Nate and Ms. Matthews for just one more minute. Alone, if you don't mind."

The reporters left and we stepped off to the side.

"How am I doing?" Ultraviolet asked, her voice much deeper and more masculine now.

"Good job," I assured Zilch. "Although the nose is a little too narrow." With a few twitches, the shape-shifter made his nose broaden ever so slightly.

"Better?" he asked.

"Perfect," I said.

He turned to my teacher. "I don't know how you see out of these things," he said with a sigh as he adjusted Ultraviolet's purple-tinted goggles.

Ms. Matthews shrugged. "Are you going to be okay if we get back to class?"

"Sure thing," Zilch promised. "I'm going to go back outside, answer one or two more questions, and then . . ." He lifted his head as if he heard a sound in the distance. "I'm sorry, but I must be going," he said, perfectly imitating the real Ultraviolet. "Someone needs my help!"

"I don't sound like that," Ms. Matthews complained.

"Oh, he's dead-on," I confirmed.

Zilch grinned. "Then I'll fly away and we'll let all the news stations run their videos and photos of the two of us together," he reassured Ms. Matthews. "After that, you'll be safely back in the good graces of the Parent-Teacher Association."

Suddenly, something occurred to me.

"Since when can you fly?" I asked Zilch.

"Phantom Ranger loaned me an experimental flight band," he replied. "I'm wearing it under my glove so no one will suspect anything."

"Zilch, I appreciate this more than you know," Ms. Matthews said.

"No big deal," he said with a laugh. "I do this all the time. When your only power is changing the way you look and sound, this is a pretty standard job. See you later!"

He headed down the hallway in the same direction the reporters had gone, leaving me alone with Ms. Matthews.

We went back into the classroom. Suddenly, Ms. Matthews lifted her head the way Zilch had just a few moments earlier.

"Okay, class," she announced. "It appears I forgot the quizzes in my mailbox up in the front office. Luckily for you, this means you have an extra five minutes to study. Don't waste it."

She walked out the door, and almost immediately, a streak of white and purple blew past the window. Less than three minutes later, Ms. Matthews returned to the classroom with a fistful of papers.

"Quiz time!" she announced with just the hint of a smile.

Check out all the action in Nate's next adventure!

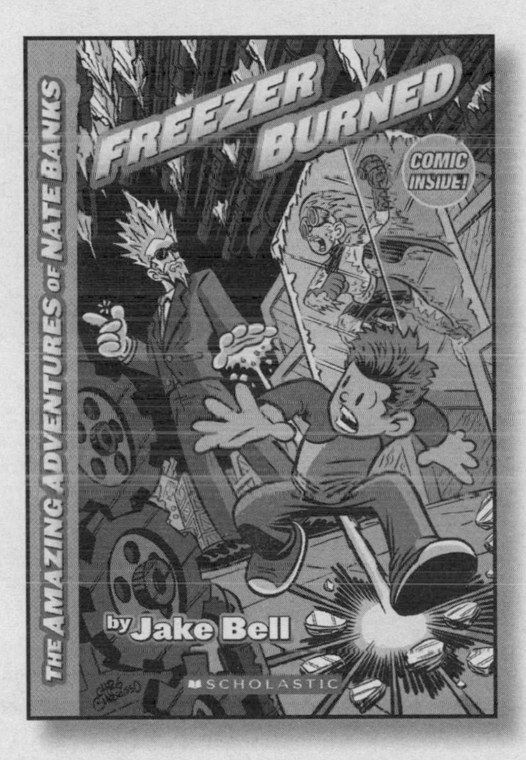

Suddenly, I noticed that the river outside the window was rotating away from the bus. In fact, the entire world was spinning around us. What could possibly be causing the bridge to spin? In an instant, I realized the world wasn't spinning—we were.

The bus driver wrestled with the steering wheel, but that had no effect. It was as though we were floating just inches off the road with no way to stop. That's not entirely accurate. There was *one* way to stop.

Perpendicular to the road, the bus hit the steel and concrete railing along the edge of the bridge. Everyone on the bus was thrown forward into the backs of the seats in front of us. A piece of the railing tore a gash in the side of the bus, narrowly missing the legs of a half dozen students.

Out my window, I could see the Moldoff River about fifty feet below. From what I could tell, the front wheels and about a third of the bus were hanging off the edge of the bridge.

"Okay, don't panic," the bus driver yelled. He stood and staggered. "We're going to have to exit out the back. One at a time! Don't push!"

One of the Eisner teachers made his way to the back and jerked the emergency handle open. Things were pretty orderly as everyone pulled themselves together and made for the exit like a sore, confused conga line.

Then the bus shifted.

Because the kids in the back got out first, the back of the bus got lighter. That meant the heavier front started to dip a little more toward the river. Everyone waiting to get out lurched backward an inch or two, but an inch or two was all it took to start a panic. Soon everyone was shoving and trying to climb over the seats to get out.

Metal groaned as the bus slid forward and the aisle became steeper. Waiting in line, I thought for the first time about Ms. Matthews. She was sitting quietly toward the front of the bus. Bracing myself against the seat backs, I clambered down to her.

"What are you doing? We need to get out—" Then I saw what she was doing. With both hands, she was gripping the steel railing that had torn through the side of the bus. By holding the railing and pushing back against the bus with her back and legs, she was preventing us from falling into the river. Or at least she was delaying our fall.

"It's not going to hold much longer, Nate," she grunted. It wasn't that she wasn't strong enough; the bus wasn't.

Only about a dozen students remained in line. I scrambled up the slope toward them. There were two other emergency doors on the sides of the bus, but one was hanging over the river and the other was smashed into the concrete railing, which is why the driver had told us—

The driver!

A quick glance toward the front of the bus confirmed

my fear. He'd never passed me on the way to the back. After telling us to get off, he had collapsed and was lying halfway down the stairs at the entrance. I rushed to help him up, Ms. Matthews shouting at me as I passed her.

Fortunately, the driver wasn't unconscious, just very dazed. With my help, he got to his feet. The last of the students were leaping out the back, so we had a clear path, though it didn't look like it was going to be easy. Every second, the slope got steeper. Both the driver and I had to pull ourselves forward using the seats like rungs on a ladder, but I also had to help support him so he didn't go tumbling to the floor each time the bus shifted.

Finally, we reached the back exit and he tried to pull himself out. With my shoulder planted in the small of his back and my legs braced against the legs of two seats, I pushed him out the door.

And then my foot slipped.